Alex's Triple Treat

Shoelaces and Brussels Sprouts
Peanut Butter and Jelly Secrets
T-Bone Trouble

Nancy Simpson

CHARIOT BOOKS
AN IMPRINT OF
CHARIOT•VICTOR PUBLISHING

Chariot•Victor Publishing
Cook Communications, Colorado Springs, CO 80918
Cook Communications, Paris, Ontario
Kingsway Communications, Eastbourne, England

ALEX'S TRIPLE TREAT

Cover design by Brad Lind
Cover illustration by Britt Taylor Collins

These stories were first published in separate editions by Chariot Books in
1987 and 1990.
First compilation printing, 1996
Printed in the USA

00 99 98 97 96   5 4 3 2 1

This book is dedicated to a few
of the many ALEX fans who have,
within the last ten years, enriched my life
with their regular correspondence.
May God bless all of you!

Sarette Albin

Missy Allen

Elizabeth Baird

Rachel Baird

Bridget Bieth

Lara Blanchard

Bonnie Brown

Heather Browne

Rachel Bright

Amber Cressman

Sarah Cromley

Becky Deckinga

Michele Ernst

Linden Hargett

Elizabeth Holden

Christine Husk

Janet Jester

Cassandra Johnson

Jenny Junkin

Kris Kraft

Kristi Kaapu

Amanda Lydon

Melissa Lydon

Roxanne McDonald

Haley Mitchell

Karla Myers

Erica Niccum

Stephanie Price

Michelle Putz

Sara Ruggles

Jenny Schipma

Tammy Schipma

Danielle Smouse

Jenny Thomas

Jennifer Weir

Elizabeth Zappulla

The ALEX Series
by Nancy Simpson Levene

- Shoelaces and Brussels Sprouts
- French Fry Forgiveness
- Hot Chocolate Friendship
- Peanut Butter and Jelly Secrets
- Mint Cookie Miracles
- Cherry Cola Champions
- The Salty Scarecrow Solution
- Peach Pit Popularity
- T-Bone Trouble
- Grapefruit Basket Upset
- Apple Turnover Treasure
- Crocodile Meatloaf
- Chocolate Chips and Trumpet Tricks
  —an Alex Devotional
- Alex's Triple Treat
  —10th Anniversary Edition

Shoelaces and Brussels Sprouts

Nancy Simpson Levene

Chariot Books
A Division of Cook Communications

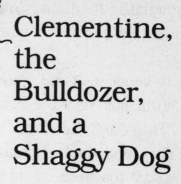

CHAPTER 1

Clementine, the Bulldozer, and a Shaggy Dog

"Hey, come on Alex! We gotta get Clementine outa there!" cried Jason.

Clementine! What a ridiculous name for a turtle, thought Alex. She peered through the fence. "Brussels sprouts!" Alex grumbled. "The last recess of the day, and I'm stuck trying to rescue a stupid turtle!"

"What'd you have to bring dumb old Clementine to school for anyway?" she hollered at Jason.

"I told you already—for show and tell. Now, do something, please!" Jason shrieked back, hopping first on one foot, then on the other.

"Okay," muttered Alex, gazing out of the fence at the turtle. Clementine, who was not

9

bothered in the least, slowly inched through the grass, now and then stopping to crunch a blade of it.

"I know! Get me a stick!" cried Alex.

Jason just stared at her dumbly.

"Hurry up! Get a big stick!"

They both looked around wildly. Jason, who was just too upset to think clearly, picked up a twig. Alex grabbed a more respectable-sized stick and jammed it through a hole in the fence.

"Too short," sighed Alex.

"Oh, no!" wailed Jason. "My turtle! My turtle!" Grabbing hold of the fence with both hands and shaking it as hard as he could, he yelled, "Clementine! You get back here!"

Oh, brussels sprouts, thought Alex. *In a minute, I suppose he'll start bawling like a baby about his old turtle! How did I ever get mixed up with this kindergartner? Ever since he moved in next door to me, he's been following me around at school. Doesn't he know better than to bother a second grader?*

"Hey, wait a minute . . . I know!" Alex suddenly exclaimed. She began pulling off her tennis shoes.

Jason, with tears just starting to run down his face, raised his head hopefully.

Alex was excited. "See, if I tie my shoelace—no, wait—if I tie both shoelaces to the stick and then throw it out, it just might be long enough. Say a prayer, kid. Here goes. . . . Oh, just a second, I gotta throw this thing over the top of the fence."

Alex started climbing the fence but stopped in amazement as she heard Jason say, "Dear Lord Jesus, please bring my turtle back to me."

"Oh, brother!" moaned Alex. "I didn't really mean he should say a prayer. Whoever heard of praying for a dumb old turtle?" She held onto the shoelaces and whirled the stick above her head a few times (just warming up) and flung it over the top of the fence. Perfect aim! What a ball player! The stick crashed right in front of Clementine, scaring the turtle so badly that it immediately turned around and ran back toward the fence.

"Grab her!" shouted Alex.

Jason shot his hand through a hole in the fence and, with a powerful stretch, caught Clementine.

"Got her!" he cried victoriously.

"Stupid turtle," muttered Alex.

"Uh, oh!" Alex gulped. A towering, massive figure in huge black boots stomped toward them, repeatedly blowing sharp blasts on a whistle.

"Double brussels sprouts! It's THE BULL-DOZER! We've had it now!" she gasped.

THE BULLDOZER, whose real name was Mrs. Peppercorn, was Alex's teacher. Alex and her friends called her THE BULLDOZER (behind her back, of course) because of her enormous size and strength.

"Oh, why, oh, why does THE BULLDOZER have to have playground duty today?" Alex could feel the school yard quieting as everyone turned to watch.

"Alexandria Brackenbury! Get off that fence!" ordered Mrs. Peppercorn. "You know you're not supposed to climb this fence! Look at you! You've got mud all over your knees and your shirt's torn. All right! What have you two been doing?"

Alex hearing her heart pounding and feeling her legs quivering, couldn't seem to open her

12

mouth. She could only stare at THE BULLDOZ-ER'S big, black boots. Those boots seemed to get bigger and bigger every second. Jason frantically clutched Clementine behind his back.

"Won't answer me, huh?" said Mrs. Pepper-corn. "Okay, you two follow me! You can spend the rest of your recess standing beside me!" THE BULLDOZER marched off, motioning them to follow at her heels.

Alex took a hurried step, but her foot came right out of her shoe. She felt mud seep into her sock.

"Brussels sprouts," she moaned, "my shoe-laces!" The stick with her laces tied to it was still on the other side of the fence. Should she go back and try to reach her shoelaces? No! Better not. THE BULLDOZER was too mad and would not understand about lost shoelaces. Besides, then she'd have to explain about Clementine, and Jason would probably get in trouble for bringing his turtle outside at recess.

Alex grumbled, "Hide that dumb turtle! THE BULLDOZER would probably make turtle soup outa her!"

Horrified, Jason crammed Clementine into one of his pockets.

Dumb, dumb, dumb, DUMB turtle! Alex's shoes flapped around her feet. Other children giggled at them. Why did kids love to see others in trouble, Alex wondered.

They reached the end of the playground where the teachers always stood and took their places by Mrs. Peppercorn. Alex stood next to her teacher and Jason stood next to Alex.

Alex glanced at Jason. He looked sick! His face was all puffy and red, and he had to keep pushing Clementine's head back down into his pocket. *What a goofy little kid,* she thought. *He's not so bad really. If only he didn't like turtles so much.* She reached over and patted his shoulder.

"Don't worry, Jason. Recess will be over soon," Alex managed to whisper. Jason looked grateful.

Standing beside THE BULLDOZER wasn't much fun, but it gave Alex time to think. "Some recess!" she exclaimed to herself. Well, actually, it had been sort of exciting. She almost giggled out loud as she remembered how funny

THE BULLDOZER had looked as she'd stomped up to them, puffing on her whistle!

Of course, she had left her shoelaces on the other side of the fence. She better get them back. Those were her special (and only) laces with little baseballs printed all over them. Brussels sprouts. If she lost them her mother would be mad! They had cost three whole dollars. Well, she could get them after school. She'd just climb the fence. . . . Boy! How about that turtle? Old Clementine had really moved fast when the stick fell in front of her . . . *hmmm* . . . that was right after Jason's prayer. Could that have had anything to do with it?

Alex looked over at Jason and Clementine. "Lord," she whispered, "do You really care about dumb, creepy turtles?"

After school, Alex and her best friend Janie hid behind a row of bushes at the side of the school building. They watched as Jason and Alex's little brother, Rudy, skipped down the sidewalk toward home. The girls planned to rescue Alex's shoelaces and didn't want the younger boys in the way. Alex waited until they were out of sight.

"Let's go!" she whispered to Janie.

The girls raced around the building to the playground.

"Okay," said Alex, "you know what to do, right?"

"Sure," answered Janie. "You climb the fence and then hand the stick with your shoelaces over to me and then you climb back over. Simple!"

"Simple!" echoed Alex. She stopped suddenly. Her feet had walked out of her shoes, and she was standing in the mud.

"Brussels sprouts! This is ridiculous! I'm just going barefoot!" She peeled her soaked socks off, rolled them into a gooey ball, and pushed them into her backpack.

"Your mother isn't going to like that," commented Janie.

"Oh, come on," shrugged Alex. She leaped and hopped the rest of the way to the fence, dodging most of the sharp rocks and missing most of the puddles.

Without waiting for Janie to catch up with her, she began climbing the fence. Ouch! The fence links hurt her bare feet.

Alex, being an excellent fence climber, was up and over before Janie even reached the fence. She only felt her jeans snag once on the spikes at the top.

"Now, where is that stick with my laces on it?" Alex looked carefully at the ground, even getting down on her hands and knees to crawl over the area. "I can't find it!" she shouted in frustration.

Janie, peering through the fence from the other side, said, "Maybe this is the wrong place. I thought you were more up that way. . . . You know, across from the swings."

"Oh," replied Alex, "maybe so." She got up and turned toward the swings. "Oh, no, look!" Alex pointed. A few yards from her was one of the biggest, shaggiest, meanest dogs she had ever seen, and it was heading right toward her. But, worst of all—Alex squinted to get a better look— in his mouth was a stick with two blue shoelaces hanging from it.

"Yikes, what do we do now?" yelled Janie.

"Shhh! You might make him mad if you yell

so loud," Alex whispered.

"He looks mad already," Janie whispered back.

Alex kept close to the fence, trying to figure how fast she could climb back over it *and* how high the dog could leap.

"Well, maybe he just looks mad but he's really friendly," whispered Alex hopefully. The dog had stopped only a few feet away and was staring at them intently.

"I don't think so," warned Janie.

"Janie, I gotta get my shoelaces!" retorted Alex ferociously.

She started inching her way toward the dog. "Nice poochie, will you give me the stick?"

"Ohhh, I can't even look," moaned Janie, covering her eyes.

The "poochie" just stared at Alex.

Brussels sprouts! thought Alex. *He's as big as I am—even bigger! And look at those teeth! Oh, wow! But those teeth are holding the stick with my shoelaces tied on it. Well, maybe he doesn't really care about the stick. Maybe I can get it.*

Alex slowly reached out one hand toward the

dog. "Grrrr," the dog growled, showing even bigger teeth.

Alex jumped back quickly!

"Get outa there!" hissed Janie.

But Alex was determined. "Those are my shoelaces!" she shouted at the dog.

"Grrrr! Ruff! Ruff!" barked the dog. He shook his head from side to side. Janie began screaming. The dog barked even louder and took a couple of steps toward Alex.

Alex, deciding she had been brave enough, leaped to the top of the fence, fully expecting the dog to nip at her toes. But the dog, quite unexpectedly, turned and bounded away. Alex was left, perched on top of the fence, to watch the dog and her shoelaces disappear.

"Brussels sprouts!" Alex was thoroughly disgusted. "Now, how am I going to get my shoelaces back?"

"Get down and let's get out of here!" Janie was thoroughly frightened.

They started for home with Janie in the lead this time. Alex didn't even feel the rocks under her bare feet. She was too upset. Luckily, she remembered to pick up her backpack.

Janie attempted to cheer up her friend. "Well, you tried, you know."

Alex didn't answer.

"Well," Janie tried again. "Your mom will buy you new shoelaces."

Alex only groaned. Her mother would never buy her *baseball* laces again. How would she understand that Alex had lost them trying to save a turtle? No, her mother would *not* understand, especially when Alex got her shoes all wet and muddy. It would have been better if the dog had bitten her in the leg and she had gone to the hospital. Then, *maybe* her mother would have felt so sorry for her that she wouldn't get mad and Alex would get new laces. Brussels sprouts!

CHAPTER 2

The First Lie

When the girls reached Alex's house, Janie called "Good luck!" and ran through the backyard. Janie lived right in back of Alex.

"Good luck, phooey," mumbled Alex. Janie could say that. She wasn't the one in all the trouble. Alex paused in front of her front door. *Maybe I shouldn't tell Mom exactly what happened.*

Bam! The door shot forward, knocking Alex to one side. A mass of arms and legs churned down the steps.

"Hey, watch where you're going!" Alex shouted.

"Oh, watch yourself, banana nose!" cried a small, blond-haired boy. This was Alex's little brother, Rudy.

Rudy's real name was David, but he had always called himself "Rudy." Only Rudy (or David) knew why. The other members of the family had given in long ago to the name change. Rudy was five years old and a major source of trouble for Alex.

Now, there he was, with his tongue sticking out of his mouth, jumping and giggling with his friends. One of the friends was Jason. How could Jason stand there and laugh at her when she'd suffered so much because of his yucky turtle? Alex glared at Jason. He quickly lost his smile. Then she turned her frown on Rudy.

"You little goblin! I'm gonna make you into meat loaf!" shrieked Alex. But before she could take even one step, she heard her mother call her.

"Alex! Is that you? You're late from school." Her mother came to the door. "Ignore your brother and come on in. Alex! What in the world has happened to you? And why are you barefoot? It's not that warm. Oh, just look at you!"

Alex looked herself over. "It's just a little mud, Mom. I, uh, fell down at recess."

Her mother was exasperated. "A little mud? You're covered with it. And your shirt's torn and missing a button, and your jeans are ripped!"

"They are?" replied Alex.

"And where are your shoes and why don't you have them on?"

"They're in my backpack," answered Alex, feeling a little exasperated herself. Too many things had gone wrong today, and now there were too many questions.

"Well, go into your bedroom and get out of those clothes. No . . . no, wait, just take them off here in the hallway. I don't need mud all over the house, and you'll have to take a bath right away!"

Alex peeled off her shirt and jeans as her mother reached into her backpack.

"Oooh, yuck!" gasped Mother as she grabbed one of Alex's slimy socks. She then pulled out the other sock and the mud-coated shoes.

"Were you wading in the creek again, Alexandria?" accused Mother. (Her mother only called her "Alexandria" when she was angry.) "I don't think I'll ever get these shoes clean. And, where are the shoelaces?''

Alex had had enough! *Mom believes I've gone in the creek. She's yellin' at me before I can even explain what happened. I was just trying to help my friend get his turtle. She's not being fair. Just for that I won't tell her how I lost my laces!*

''No, I didn't go in the creek,'' Alex told her mother, ''and I, uh, loaned my shoelaces to Janie, uh, 'cause she needed them for gym class and hers broke.'' LIAR! screamed a voice inside of her. Alex's face felt hot and her legs started shaking strangely, but she didn't correct the lie.

Her mother just looked at her for what seemed like a long time. Then, shrugging her shoulders, Mother gathered up the clothes and walked away.

In the bathtub, Alex scrunched down until the water reached her chin. She was miserable. She hadn't even bothered to make purple bubbles from her giant plastic softball bubble bath container.

Brussels sprouts! I shouldn't have said that to Mom, she thought. Alex couldn't remember ever telling her mother such a straight-out lie. Well, there was the time she'd said that Rudy broke her favorite miniature glass horse. (She'd paid a whole dollar for it at the carnival.) Rudy *had* fallen against her dresser and knocked it off. Of course, Alex had first shoved him into the dresser.

"Maybe I should go tell Mom what really happened," Alex said to herself. "No, I'd just get in more trouble for lying. Anyway, Mom really wasn't very fair. She thought I went into the creek and I didn't!" Alex kicked the water, splashing some out of the tub.

Alex gave the water a couple more good kicks. *So . . . maybe if she thinks I'm so bad,* she thought angrily, *I'll just be bad. But lying is wrong,* she reminded herself. *It's a sin. God won't like it.*

"Oh, I don't know what to do," sighed Alex. She ducked her face under water and blew bubbles.

"Rudy! Sit up straight and quit wiggling," Mother ordered.

"Yes," agreed Father. "The dinner table is not the place to do cartwheels and somersaults."

Rudy giggled, "You mean I shouldn't do this?" He turned upside down in his chair. Father quickly grabbed a kicking foot an inch above the mashed potato bowl.

"I give up," sighed Mother.

Mom says that a lot, thought Alex. *I hope she never really gives up.* Alex wasn't too sure just what her mother meant by "giving up." She didn't want her to give up anything. Unless, of course, it was Rudy.

Dinner was almost over. Roast beef, mashed potatoes, broccoli, and applesauce. What a dull dinner! Alex wondered why they couldn't have something exciting—like hot dogs or pizza.

"Mmmm, this is yummy!" remarked Alex's older sister, Barbara. She daintily spooned another helping of potatoes onto her plate and shaped them into a smooth, miniature mountain. Barbara then made a perfectly round little hole in the top of her mountain. She carefully filled it almost to the top with gravy.

Alex wished that just once her mountain would leak. She sat very still concentrating on Barbara's potato mountain, hoping to see brown juice ooze out the sides. But she was disappointed. It didn't leak.

Miss Perfect! Barbara never does anything wrong. She sure doesn't get into messes like me. I bet she's never told a lie. She's always kind and polite and . . . what does Mom say? Oh, yeah, "mature for her age." Alex wasn't quite sure what that meant. It had something to do with acting grown up. To Alex, Barbara *was* grown up. After all, her sister was twelve and in the sixth grade.

Mom sometimes would ask Alex why she couldn't be more like her sister. Brussels sprouts! How could she be like her sister? She was Alex, not Barbara! Anyway, her sister never did anything exciting. All she wanted to do was wash her hair, talk on the phone, listen to goofy records, and put on that awful, hot pink nail polish.

"Hey, Firecracker!" boomed her father, leaning across the table. "What's the matter? You haven't said two words all through dinner."

Her father always called Alex "Firecracker." He had special nicknames for all his children. He called Barbara "Princess" and he called Rudy

"Steam Roller." Alex also had special nick-
names for her brother and sister. She called
Barbara "Miss Mushy" and she called Rudy
"Goblin."

"I have so said two words, Dad," Alex answered. "I've said *more* than two words!"

"Well, excuuuse me," apologized Father. He
made a low bow and pretended to crash his
forehead on the table. Alex had to giggle. Dad
could be so funny!

"Please tell me, my dearest Firecracker,"
asked her father, "what two words did you

favor us with?''

"Well, just awhile ago," answered Alex, "I said 'please pass the butter.' ''

Hoots and hollers of laughter came from her father, mother, and sister.

"Well, what's so funny?'' demanded Alex. "That's more than two words. That's four words!''

They all laughed again. Alex sighed. *Grownups! I'll never understand them.*

After dinner was finally over, Alex ran upstairs to her bedroom and closed the door. She needed a quiet place. She had some thinking to do. Unfortunately, no one else in her family understood.

"Alex! ALEX!'' cried Rudy. "You wanna race Big Wheels?'' Sometimes, when Alex felt she could stand being around Rudy, they would speed around the driveway on their "motorcycles.''

She flung open her door. "No!'' she yelled down the stairway. "Go away, Goblin!'' She slammed her door shut again.

Her mother immediately opened it. "Alexandria! There was no reason to yell at your brother like that. That was rude. What is the matter with you tonight?''

''Nothing,'' Alex told her. She climbed on her bed and hugged her stuffed cat, Garfield.

Mother left the room.

As Alex lay on the bed holding her cat, her thoughts returned to her shoelaces. *What can I do? I gotta have shoelaces.*

Her sister's voice interrupted her thoughts. ''Alex! Hey, Alex! Your favorite show's on TV. Don't you want to watch it?''

Alex yanked her door open again. ''No, thank you, Miss Mushy,'' she called sweetly (a little too sweetly). Her mother, who was standing in the upstairs hallway, gave her a frown.

Alex banged her door shut. ''How can anyone think around here?'' she moaned.

Her door opened again. Thinking it was Barbara, Alex cried, ''I don't wanna watch TV! Leave me alone!'' Her mother stood in the doorway.

Mother gave Alex a long look. She said quietly, ''I've washed your shoes, Alex. Here they are. They're a little wet, but they should dry by morning.'' Mother turned and left, closing the door softly.

Alex stared at the door for a long time. "I am mean and ugly," she told herself. "I yelled at Mom and I lied to her and I'm afraid to tell her the truth." She slowly sank to the floor. Alex felt guilty.

"Hey, Firecracker!" she heard her father call. Alex didn't feel like getting up.

"FIRECRACKER!" That call was much louder. She had better answer. She didn't need Dad angry with her, too.

Alex sighed and opened her door. Before she could answer, her father called up the stairs. "Janie's on the telephone."

Janie! Oh, good! Talking to her best friend would surely help. Alex rushed into Barbara's room to answer the phone.

"Hello," she said.

"Hi," answered Janie. "Did you tell your mom about your shoelaces? Are you in trouble?"

"Well, not exactly," replied Alex.

"You mean she didn't get mad?"

"No . . . I mean I didn't tell her," Alex stated.

"Oh . . . you mean she didn't even notice?"

Janie sounded surprised.

Alex looked up. Her mother was standing in the doorway.

"Alex," said Mother, "tell Janie not to forget to bring your shoelaces to school tomorrow. You'll need them."

"Uh, okay," said Alex to her mother.

"Alex? Alex, are you still there?" Janie's voice shouted over the telephone.

"Well, tell her right now so you don't forget," suggested Mother.

"Okay! Uh, Janie, my mom says not to forget my shoelaces in the morning!"

"Huh?" asked Janie. "What are you talking about?"

"I said," repeated Alex, "don't forget my shoelaces in the morning!" She glanced at her mother. Mother nodded her head and left the doorway.

"Have you gone crazy?" yelled Janie. "I don't have your laces! The dog has them! Don't you remember?"

Alex hissed into the phone, "Of course, I remember!" She then tried to explain to Janie all that had happened.

Janie was amazed. "You mean you told your mom that you gave your shoelaces to me for my gym class? That's looney! Alex, how could you say that? Now, when you don't have your laces tomorrow she'll blame me!"

"No, she won't," Alex tried to reassure Janie. "Don't worry, I'll think of something."

"Well, you better think of telling her the truth!" snapped Janie and hung up.

Back in her room, Alex slowly undressed and pulled her Incredible-Hulk-holding-up-a-building pajama top over her head. Mother had bought the pajamas especially for her in the boys' department. Alex hated nightgowns. Such silly, sissy things. They didn't even keep your legs warm!

Alex turned out the light and crawled into bed with Garfield.

Pretty soon her door opened and a shadow walked across the room and sat down on the edge of her bed. It was Mother. "Alex, honey, do you feel all right?" she asked.

"Yeah," mumbled Alex.

"You didn't give me a good-night kiss," reminded her mother. She bent over and kissed Alex's forehead. "You know you can always talk to me when something's wrong," Mother suggested gently.

I can't this time, thought Alex, *cuz I lied to you.* But all she said was, "I'm okay."

Mother tried again. "Would you like for me to listen to your prayers?"

"No," replied Alex, "I'd rather say them by myself tonight."

"Okay, sweetheart. Just remember that I love you very much," said her mother and gave her another kiss.

Father strode into the room. "And I love you, too, my little Firecracker. Maybe tomorrow evening you'll say more to me than 'please pass the butter.' " He walked over to her bed and gave Alex a good-night kiss.

After Mother and Father left the room, Alex lay in bed remembering the whole day. She thought about Clementine's rescue and suddenly got an idea. *Maybe if the Lord cares enough to help Jason get his dumb ol' turtle back, well, then maybe He'll help me, too.*

She rolled off her bed and got on her knees. "Dear Lord Jesus," she prayed, "if You're not too mad at me for telling a lie, will You help me get my shoelaces back?"

CHAPTER 3

Cowboy Boot Catastrophe

"Alex! Hurry up! You will be late for school!" called Mother from downstairs.

"Coming!" Alex yelled back. "Ouch!" She winced as she pulled and tugged her old cowboy boots onto her feet. There were just no other shoes to wear. She had scrounged around in her closet and had only found her winter snow boots, her dress shoes, and her cowboy boots.

"Alex! Come on!" Mother sounded frustrated.

Alex bounded down the stairs and landed with a crash at the bottom. *Boy, these boots are sure noisy,* she thought. She grabbed her sweat shirt from a hook and flung open the front door.

"Wait a minute, don't forget your lunch," called Mother.

Alex ran into the kitchen.

"I hope you put your tennis shoes in your backpack," said Mother. "You know you have softball practice after school." She was looking at Alex's feet. "I don't think your coach would appreciate those boots!"

"Oh, yeah," mumbled Alex. She raced back up the stairs.

Thump, thump, thump, crash! She was back down again, hurriedly stuffing her shoes in her backpack.

"I wonder where Janie is?" questioned her mother. "She's usually here by now to walk to school with you."

"Oh," replied Alex, "well, maybe she had to go early or something."

"Hmmmm, maybe," was all Mother said.

Alex quickly kissed her mother good-bye and stumbled down the front steps. "I can't even walk in these boots," Alex complained. She hobbled to the side of her house and peered around the corner at the backyard. No, she didn't see Janie. "Where is she? She can't still be mad, can she? We always walk to school together!

Maybe she's sick. That's it!" Alex hobbled a little farther down the sidewalk. "No, Janie's probably not sick. She's probably still mad." Alex felt awful. She walked with her head down, staring at the sidewalk.

"Hi!" a voice suddenly shouted.

"Aaaaah!" Alex jumped straight in the air.

"I've been waiting here behind this tree for a long time," complained Janie. "Where have you been?"

"I got a late start," Alex gulped. "Boy, I didn't even see you!"

"Well, I was hiding," Janie explained. "I didn't want your mom to see me. . . . You know, cuz of the shoelaces."

"Oh, yeah, brussels sprouts."

"Come on, we better get going. We might be late," warned Janie. She hurried up the street. Alex limped beside her.

The two girls reached school just as the morning bell started to ring. They clambered up the steps and raced down the hall.

"See you at recess!" they both called to each other. Janie turned into one room, and Alex raced into the next. Alex slid across the floor and into her desk with a bang just as the bell quit ringing. THE BULLDOZER frowned and stared at her for a full minute.

The room was silent. Alex could hear the birds twittering outside and the clock ticking inside (or was that her heart beating?).

"Alexandria!" growled Mrs. Peppercorn. "Since you are so *eager* to get to school today, perhaps you'd like to be the first one to do a math problem on the blackboard."

Alex groaned and looked at the blackboard. Subtraction! The kind where the ones' column had to borrow from the tens' column. The worst kind!

"Well?" Mrs. Peppercorn tapped her foot.

Alex jumped up and bumped into her desk. A book fell off and crashed to the floor. Alex reached down to pick it up and hit her desk again. A pencil slid off her desk and rolled under it. Alex dove for her pencil, lost her balance and fell on the floor under her desk.

The whole room howled with laugher! It took THE BULLDOZER a long time to quiet the classroom down.

Alex lay on the floor clutching her pencil. She couldn't move. She was frozen with fear.

"Alexandria!" called her teacher. "It will be a little difficult to do your math problem when you are lying *under* a desk!"

"Oh, why can't I just disappear," moaned Alex. She wondered how many seconds it would take to dash across the room and out the door.

Alex risked a glance at her teacher. She was smiling! THE BULLDOZER was actually smiling! Alex sheepishly smiled back and crawled out from under her desk. She stumbled up to the blackboard. Giggles and snickers followed her all the way.

"Ahem," Mrs. Peppercorn cleared her throat and the giggles ceased.

"Alexandria, you may do problem number one. Everyone pay attention! I may call on you to do the next one," Mrs. Peppercorn warned the class.

Eighty-one minus 57. Hmmmm, let's see. I can't subtract 7 from 1. Brussels Sprouts! Why is all this crazy stuff happening to me? . . . Twenty-

four! The answer is 24! She turned and looked at her teacher triumphantly.

"Very good, Alexandria," said Mrs. Peppercorn. "You may take your seat now. Jeffrey, up to the blackboard and answer the second problem."

Alex almost skipped back to her desk. *Wow, she thought, THE BULLDOZER told me "very good" and she smiled at me. That's great! Now, if I can just figure out what to do about my shoelaces, this could turn into a good day.*

"BATTER UP!" yelled Mr. Glover. "Alex! This time, for pete's sake, get the ball over the plate!"

"Okay, Coach," Alex yelled back. She was having a lot of trouble with her pitching this afternoon at ball practice. All because of her cowboy boots. She looked down at her feet. Brussels sprouts! Her boots kept slipping in the grass and dirt and throwing her off balance so that her pitches were wild. "I probably can't even outrun Fat Lorraine," she grumbled to herself. Fat Lorraine was the worst player and the slowest runner on the team.

Alex got ready for the next pitch. She made a little slice in the dirt and stomped the heel of her right foot in it. Maybe that would hold it steady. She drew her right arm way back, stepped forward on her left foot, swung her right arm forward, and let the ball go. Her foot didn't slip this time.

"Strike one!" hollered Mr. Glover.

"Way to go," she told herself. She dug her heel in again and threw another pitch.

"Strike two! Good going, Alex!" her coach cried again. "Come on, Sally," he told the batter, "don't just look at the ball!"

Sally looked disgusted. "How was I supposed to know she'd finally throw two good pitches? She's been throwing them over the backstop all day!"

"Very funny," muttered Alex. "I've only thrown three pitches *over* the backstop. These miserable boots!" She caught the ball from the catcher and dug her heel in the same spot. She wound up and stepped forward, but as the ball was leaving her hand, the dirt in front of her right foot gave way. Her foot slipped. The ball flew straight up in the air. It hit the edge of the top of the backstop and came bounding straight back at Alex. She jumped in the air to catch it. The ball hit her fingertips with enough force to tilt her backwards. As she came down from her jump, her boots slipped right out from under her. Alex landed flat on her back in the dirt!

As Alex lay there on her back, she heard Mr. Glover yell, "Strike three!"

She lifted her head. Had Sally really swung at that pitch? Sally had, and it was hard to tell whether their coach was more disgusted with Alex or Sally. He just gazed in amazement at both of them. He finally shook his head and walked off the field. "That's enough for today," he shouted and threw his hands in the air.

Alex yanked her boots off and threw them across the field. Brussels sprouts! She started drawing circles in the dirt. "Those boots have caused me a lot of trouble today," she reflected.

"Alex!" said a loud voice. She looked up to see Mr. Glover striding toward her. He was carrying her boots. He dropped them in the dirt

and squatted down beside her.

"I hope you realize that ball practice is no place for cowboy boots," he said gruffly. Alex nodded.

"Remember," her coach went on, "we've got our first big game coming up on Saturday." He looked at her. Alex nodded again. His voice softened, "You know we're not playing tee ball anymore, and I need my star pitcher in good form." He gave her a pat on the back and walked away.

Alex stood up slowly and brushed the dirt off

her jeans. She turned each boot upside down to pour out the dirt. She pulled them back on her feet, picked her backpack up, and headed for home.

CHAPTER 4

Two More Lies and a Gutter Pipe Lie

When Alex reached her house after ball practice she ran around to the backyard. "If I take my backpack inside with my tennis shoes in it then Mom will see that I still don't have my shoelaces," she told herself. "I better hide it!"

Alex looked around and picked out a small bush in a corner of the yard. She made sure no one was watching her. She quickly stuffed her backpack underneath the bush. Then she darted around to the front of the house and stomped inside.

Her mother was scurrying around in the kitchen, banging lids on pans.

Alex tried sneaking down the hallway and up the stairs to her bedroom.

"Alex?" Mother called from the kitchen.

Darn these noisy boots, Alex thought for at least the one hundredth time that day.

"Yeah?" Alex answered without moving.

Mother came out of the kitchen, wiping her hands on a dish towel. "Alex, how was school today?"

"Okay," answered Alex. She climbed up a couple more steps.

"Well . . . how was ball practice?"

"Okay," sighed Alex. She was certain more questions were coming.

Sure enough, her mother asked another one. "Aren't you going to take your sweat shirt off before going upstairs?"

"Oh, yeah." Alex clattered down the steps and hung her sweat shirt on a hook by the front door.

"Did you wear those boots to ball practice?" exclaimed Mother.

Brussels sprouts! I knew she'd ask that question, thought Alex. *Now what do I do? If I say "yes" then she'll just get mad like the coach.*

"Huh?" Alex asked. Maybe if she waited long enough to answer, something would happen—

like the meat loaf would blow up in the oven and Mom would have to run into the kitchen.

The meat loaf did not blow up, and her mother again asked if she'd worn her boots to ball practice.

"Oh, uh, well, kinda," Alex stammered. "I just wanted to see how they'd work," she quickly added.

"Uh, huh," said Mother, "and how did they work?"

"Terrible!" exclaimed Alex.

"Where are your tennis shoes?"

"In my backpack," Alex said. *So far,* she thought, *I haven't told her another lie. My tennis shoes are in my backpack and I did sorta want to see if I could pitch in my boots.* Still, Alex could feel her face getting hot, and her legs were beginning to quiver. She started moving up the stairs hoping to end the questions. It didn't work.

"Okay," said her mother in an exasperated tone, "your shoes are in your backpack. Now, where is your backpack?"

Brussels sprouts! How do mothers learn to ask all these questions? How can I say I hid it in the backyard under a bush?

Alex turned her head away from her mother and said in a rush, "I left it at school. I'll get it tomorrow." She ran up the stairs, into her bedroom, and slammed her door shut.

After a while, Alex heard her mother call her name. "Come on, Alex, it's time to eat dinner."

"Dinner?" cried Alex. "Isn't it too early for dinner?"

"Not if you want to eat before you go to choir practice," Mother called. "Now, hurry up! Jason's mother is driving all of you to the church tonight, and we don't want to make her wait."

"Okay," sighed Alex. She ran down the stairs. Choir practice. She'd forgotten about that.

At the table, Alex gulped down her dinner, trying to ignore Rudy's silliness.

Soon a car horn beeped from the driveway. "Yahoo! Jason's here!" shouted Rudy. He ran to the door.

"Get your jackets!" cried Mother.

All three children hurried out to the car.

"Rudy! Please quit kicking Janet's chair! Jason, I can't talk when you're talking! Now children, we have a lot of work to do. You know we sing at the church service in two weeks and—eeeeek! Ooooh!'' Mrs. Williams, the choir director, slapped a hand to her chest and pointed at the floor. She quickly backed away from her music stand.

''Hey, look! A turtle!'' shouted a boy in the front row.

''Oh, wow! Clementine got out!'' cried Jason. He ran to the front of the room to grab his turtle. Clementine was plodding around Mrs. Williams's music stand.

''Jason!'' gasped Mrs. Williams. ''Is *that* yours? It seemed as if Mrs. Williams would jump on the piano if Clementine got any closer to her.

''A turtle! A turtle!'' Total confusion erupted as chairs scraped and banged into each other. Most of the children rushed forward to see Clementine.

Alex was not one of them. She had no desire to meet Clementine again. She stayed in her chair, with her head in her hands, and moaned, ''Not that stupid turtle again!''

Rudy, on the other hand, was delighted. "Jason! Ya got any more turtles?" he yelled, dashing to the front of the room.

"Don't step on her!" screamed Jason. One eager boy pushed by another and staggered dangerously close to Clementine. To avoid squishing the turtle, the boy hurtled forward and crashed into the music stand. Music flew everywhere!

Seeing her music fluttering around the room was enough reason for Mrs. Williams to risk getting a little closer to Clementine. She quickly rescued her music and picked up the stand.

Jason grabbed Clementine.

"Children!" Mrs. Williams cried in all the excitement. "Quiet!" The accompanist banged several bass chords on the piano.

"I SAID, 'QUIET!' " yelled Mrs. Williams.

The room full of children slowly settled down. Only a few giggles were heard.

"Jason, I do not appreciate this one bit. Go find a box or something to put that creature in!" ordered Mrs. Williams.

Jason and Clementine hurried out of the room and the choir began rehearsing. Alex turned her

thoughts to her own problems. *I told another lie to Mom today,* she thought sadly. *Brussels sprouts! I just gotta find a way to get more shoelaces. Then everything will be okay and I won't have to lie any—*

"Alex! ALEX!" Mrs. Williams called.

The girl next to Alex nudged her.

"What?" said Alex, raising her head.

"Alex," said Mrs. Williams. "Please join your group over by the piano. We are going to practice our two-part song."

"Oh, yeah, okay," mumbled Alex. She got up

to go to her group. She had to walk sideways through a row of chairs and didn't notice that it was Rudy's row until it was too late. Rudy tripped her!

BANG! CRASH! Alex fell into the next row of chairs. Rudy and his friends howled with laughter.

"GOBLIN!" screeched Alex. She jumped on Rudy, who wasn't fast enough to get out of her way. They both smashed to the floor in a heap.

"ALEX, RUDY!" shouted Mrs. Williams. She rushed over to them. Alex, by now, had Rudy pinned to the floor.

"You ever do that again, Goblin, and I'll squash you into mush!" hissed Alex. She bounced on Rudy's stomach a few times to show him that she meant business.

Mrs. Williams pulled Alex off of Rudy. "Alex and Rudy, stop it this instant! Rudy, get up off the floor."

Mrs. Williams looked from Rudy to Alex. "Don't you know what our Lord says about fighting? If someone hurts you, you should not hurt him back. That would make your actions just as wrong as his.''

"The Lord," sulked Alex, "did not have a little brother like Rudy!''

"Alex!" Mrs. Williams exclaimed. "The Bible tells us that Jesus, when He was living on earth, had four little brothers!''

"He did?" Alex cried. "How awful!''

Mrs. Williams chuckled. "If that seems like too many brothers, Alex, think about this. We are all brothers and sisters to Jesus!''

"*All* of us?" Alex replied. "Boy, does He ever have His hands full!''

Everyone laughed.

When all was quiet, Mrs. Williams said, "We are taught in God's Word not to fight even when someone else hurts us.'' She looked at Rudy. "We are also not supposed to start a fight.'' Rudy looked down at the floor.

"Tell me, Alex, what did Jesus do when the soldiers nailed Him to the cross?" Mrs. Williams asked. "That must have hurt Him terribly to have nails hammered through His hands and feet.''

"Yeah," Alex agreed.

"Did He do anything to those soldiers for

hurting Him?'' Mrs. Williams asked again.

"No," answered Alex.

Mrs. Williams smiled. "You're right, Alex. Jesus didn't hurt the soldiers even though they were hurting Him. But there is something He did do for the soldiers," stated Mrs. Williams. "What was it?"

Alex thought for a moment. "Oh, yeah, I know!" she cried. "Jesus forgave them!"

"Very good! We need to follow Jesus' example and forgive others when they hurt us." Mrs. Williams gave Alex a hug.

After choir practice, Alex lay on her bedroom floor. "I should be getting ready for bed, but Mom will be busy with Rudy for a while. Oh, how I wish I hadn't told another lie today. How am I ever gonna get more shoelaces?" She stared at the ceiling. "What I could do is buy some more laces myself. If I had enough money." Alex knew that she didn't have enough money. She'd spent all that she had on a new pitcher's mitt. Brussels sprouts! Alex went back to staring at the ceiling.

Soon she heard footsteps on the stairway and

then in the upstairs hallway. Her sister's bedroom door opened and then closed. Suddenly, Alex had an idea. She got up and walked over to her sister's room. Alex tapped on the door.

"Yes?" called Barbara.

Alex opened the door and stepped inside. "Miss Mu—I mean Barbara, may I borrow some money from you?" Alex asked in her nicest voice. "I'll pay you back," she added quickly.

"How much?" asked Barbara.

"Three dollars," Alex answered.

"What for?" questioned Barbara.

"Uh, I just need it," Alex stated.

"Not good enough, Squirt," said Barbara. "If you want me to give you three whole dollars, you have to tell me why."

Alex stared at her sister. "I can't tell you. It's a secret."

"Okay, kid, but you won't get the money that way," replied her sister.

Alex stomped her foot. Miss Mushy was being difficult. She just had to get the three dollars. But she couldn't tell the real reason why she needed it. Miss Mushy would just go blab it all to Mom.

Alex thought for a moment.

"Uh," she said, "well, you know Mom's birthday is coming up soon."

"Yeah, it's this Sunday."

It is? thought Alex. *That was soon!* She tried not to look surprised.

"Well?" asked Barbara.

"Well," echoed Alex. "I want to buy a present."

"Is that what you need the three dollars for, Alex?" Barbara asked.

Alex gulped. Another lie? "Yes!" she answered quickly. She couldn't look directly at her sister. Alex had the same awful feeling now as when she had lied to her mother.

Barbara looked at Alex. "Where's all that money you got for your birthday?"

"Spent it on my pitcher's mitt," Alex replied.

"Oh, brother," sighed Barbara.

"But I really need it," explained Alex.

Barbara threw up her hands and grabbed her purse off the bed. She took three dollars out of her billfold and handed them to Alex.

"Thanks!" cried Alex and sprinted out the

bedroom door.

"I want it back, kid, and soon!" Barbara called after her.

Alex skipped all around her room. She felt that her troubles were over. Alone, in bed, she thanked the Lord Jesus for helping her find a way to get some more shoelaces. She thought surely the Lord was helping her—after all, it had been so *easy* to get the three dollars. What did it matter that she had lied to her sister? She would buy new laces tomorrow and then, somehow, find a way to pay back Miss Mushy.

The next morning Alex leaped out of bed early. She pulled on her clothes and picked up her boots. She tiptoed down the stairs in her socks and sneaked quickly out the back door. Outside, she paused to jam her feet into her boots. Oh, ow! They really hurt! "Oh, well, this is the last day I have to wear them," she told herself. She hobbled over to the bush where her backpack was hidden. She looked under the bush. There it was. Right where she had left it. She picked it up. "Why do I need to carry these shoes around all day? I can leave them out here 'til after school.

Then I can bring them inside with the new laces in 'em that I'm gonna buy.''

Alex started to push her shoes back under the bush but then remembered the mean, ugly dog who had stolen her shoelaces. "Brussels sprouts! I need a safer place to hide them." Alex looked around. She noticed the gutter pipe that ran along the edge of the roof and down a corner of the house. "A perfect hiding place!"

She ran over to the opening. Was it big enough? She peered into it. She grabbed one shoe and, with a few hard pushes, shoved it in and up through the curve in the pipe. Now for the other one. She pushed and shoved with all her might. It finally went in, too. "I don't think any dog can get 'em out of there," she told herself. "But I better make sure." She searched the backyard for just the right-sized rock. She found one and wedged it in front of her shoe. Good job!

Alex left her backpack at the side of the house where she was sure her mother wouldn't see it. She opened the back door and went inside.

Brussels sprouts! Her father was standing right by the door. Had he seen her hiding her shoes outside in the gutter pipe?

"Well, well . . . I wondered who was coming through my door so early this morning. Tell me, Firecracker, were you out for your morning jog?" joked her father.

Alex was too startled to reply. She felt her face turn red.

"Let's see, if not for a jog, perhaps you were doing a bit of early bird watching?" asked her father. "Tell me, did you see any red-tailed fincharookas?"

Alex decided Dad couldn't have seen her hiding her shoes. He would not be joking around so much if he had.

"No, no fincharookas," answered Alex. She felt she had to explain why she'd been outside. "I was just out seeing what kind of day it was—you know, if it was hot or cold," she told him. "I gotta get ready for school now!"

In her rush, Alex didn't really notice that she had lied to her father. Lying was getting easier and easier.

CHAPTER 5

A
Stormy
Lie

After breakfast, Alex grabbed up her backpack from the side of the house and walked down the sidewalk.

Janie was waiting for Alex behind the same tree. "I'll sure be glad when I can come to your house again," she told Alex wistfully.

"After today, you can!" Alex announced joyfully.

"You mean you're finally gonna tell your mom the truth?" Janie asked hopefully. Alex winced. Janie made her feel guilty all over again.

"No!" she shouted at Janie. "I've thought of a way to get new shoelaces!"

Janie stared at her.

"See," Alex explained, "if I buy new laces just like the old ones and put them in my shoes,

Mom will never know the difference!''

Janie looked doubtful. She said, ''New shoe-laces always look cleaner and better than old ones.''

''Oh, I'll just tell Mom that you washed 'em after you borrowed 'em,'' shrugged Alex. She explained how the two of them were going to go to a store after school and buy new shoelaces.

''Ridiculous!'' shouted Janie. ''Alex! How are we going to buy shoelaces ourselves? I've never been to a store by myself.''

''Look,'' she told Janie, ''there's a drugstore two streets down from the school. After school we can run there and buy the laces. It won't take long. It'll be easy!''

Janie was not reassured. ''My mom would kill me if she knew I went to that store by myself.''

''She'll never know. Besides, you won't be by yourself,'' yelled Alex. ''You'll be with me!''

Alex was tired of doing math papers. She'd finished three of them while she was waiting for THE BULLDOZER to call her reading group.

She laid her pencil down on the desk and

looked out the window. Huge black clouds were rolling across the sky. *Oh, yuck,* Alex thought to herself. More rain meant more mud and puddles on the playground and softball field. She thought of the trouble she'd had yesterday trying to pitch in her boots. She didn't even want to think what her coach would say if she showed up in cowboy boots again.

"Reading group one!" shouted Mrs. Peppercorn. The shout made Alex jump in her seat. She scrambled out of her desk and rushed to the reading corner, carrying her reading book. CLUMP, CLUMP, CLUMP went Alex's boots as she hurried to a safe chair (three down from THE BULLDOZER). *I wonder why no one else in this class wears cowboy boots?* She wished that she weren't the only noisy one.

"Alex!" her teacher said sternly, "I hope you brought suitable shoes for gym class."

Brussels sprouts! She had forgotten all about gym class. She stared down at her boots and didn't answer. She knew she couldn't wear boots inside on the gymnasium floor. Well, maybe they would have gym outside today. She glanced out the window. No way! It was blacker than ever. *Looks like it's gonna pour,* thought Alex.

THE BULLDOZER picked the girl to her left to start reading aloud which meant that Alex would be the third one to read. "Better pay attention," she told herself.

Just as the story began, lightning and thunder began outside. Flash! CRASH! Flash! CRASH! *Wow, just like giant fireworks!* thought Alex. The windows were rattling as sheets of rain hit them. The lights flickered.

What a storm! Alex couldn't keep her eyes away from the windows. *I sure hope it clears up after school,* Alex said to herself. *I'll have extra trouble getting Janie to the store in a thunderstorm. Boy, I'm glad I found such a neat hiding place for my shoes. The rain gutter is perfect. . . . No one'll find 'em there. Brussels sprouts!* Alex sat straight up in her chair.

The rain gutter! My shoes will be soaked; maybe even ruined! She groaned out loud. *Well, maybe they won't be ruined,* she told herself. *After all, they always get wet in the washing machine.*

"Alex! ALEX!" Mrs. Peppercorn called.

Alex gazed at her teacher and blinked her eyes. "Huh?" was all she could answer.

"It's your turn to read. Are you back from the galaxies now?" THE BULLDOZER looked annoyed.

"Oh," replied Alex. Her face turned red. She looked at her book. She started reading.

"Alexandria!" Mrs. Peppercorn said sharply. "All the rest of us are on page twenty-two. You may begin at the top of the page." There were giggles.

Brussels, brussels, brussels—Alex's fingers fumbled at the page corners—sprouts! She found page twenty-two and once more began reading.

As children stampeded through hallways, Alex searched frantically for Janie. She caught a glimpse of the front doorway. Someone was standing there in a bright red coat. Janie had a red raincoat. Was that her? Alex pushed and shoved her way to the door.

"Janie!" she cried in relief. She should have known Janie wouldn't leave her. Best friends didn't do that.

"Alex," Janie said nervously, "I still don't think this is such a good idea."

"I gotta get 'em, Janie!" Alex answered.

"But it's pouring down rain!"

"Oh, come on. It's just water." Alex grabbed her friend's hand and pulled her down the steps and headed in the direction of the store.

Suddenly, she heard a very familiar voice calling her name. "Alex! Alex!" Alex looked toward the street. Her mother was leaning out the window of their station wagon, motioning Alex to get in the car. Rudy was already sitting in the front seat of the car.

Alex looked at Janie and Janie looked at Alex. Then they both stood in the middle of the sidewalk and stared at Alex's mother. What was she doing here? Within a few seconds they were completely soaked from the rain, but they were so surprised to see Alex's mother that they couldn't move.

"Alex! Janie! Don't just stand there! Get in the car!" Mother sounded impatient.

Alex hesitated further. What she really wanted to do was dash down the sidewalk to the store. She looked to her right. No, she'd never make it. Mom would catch her. Besides, it was raining so hard she couldn't even see the end of the block.

"Right now!" Mother ordered.

"Brussels sprouts!" Alex pulled Janie to the car and jumped in the backseat. Janie, however, stayed outside.

"I can walk," she told Alex's mother.

"Janie, don't be ridiculous! Get in here!" said Mother in her most stern voice.

Janie quickly got in beside Alex.

Mother faced both of them. "I told your moth-

er, Janie, that I would pick you up." She gave
each of them one of her long looks. Then she
said, "I don't understand why you both just stood
out there in the rain! Why didn't you come to the
car immediately?" Mother's voice got louder
with each word. She wasn't finished yet.

"Why," Mother went on, "were you two
heading in the opposite direction from home?"
She was almost shouting now. Alex rarely saw
her mother get so angry.

"Well? Answer me!" Mother demanded.

Alex and Janie cringed in the backseat. Even
Rudy was silent.

Alex knew she had to say something. "We
were going . . . to take a shortcut," she said in a
small voice. Janie looked at Alex with a surprised
face, but she kept still.

"A shortcut?" exclaimed Mother. "How can
you take a shortcut if you're walking in the wrong
direction?"

"I don't know," answered Alex. "We just
thought there might be one that way."

Mother stared at Alex in a way that Alex hadn't
seen very often. *She looks like she doesn't believe*

me, thought Alex. That hurt! Alex was filled again with guilt.

Her mother finally turned around and started the car. "Well," she said quietly. "I don't know either, Alex. I just don't know!"

The ride home seemed incredibly long. Maybe it was because no one was talking. No one except Rudy and he wasn't really talking—just making weird sounds as he flew his airplane around the car.

They finally reached Janie's house and let her out. They drove around to their own house and pulled into the garage.

As Mother began pulling the garage door down, Alex slipped underneath it and dashed outside.

"Alex!" cried her mother. "What are you doing?"

The door was halfway down so Alex bent over and yelled under it, "I'm going in the backyard for a minute!"

Rudy must have thought that was a great idea. He, too, dashed under the door and outside.

"Rudy!" Mother yelled. She pushed the garage door all the way up again.

"Get in here both of you!" shouted Mother. Rudy was leaping around in the rain, shouting with glee at every thunder crash.

Mother rushed out of the garage, grabbed Rudy's arm and dragged him inside. Alex followed.

"I'm sorry, Mom," she said meekly.

Mother banged the door down. She didn't answer Alex. She just pointed to the door. Alex and Rudy marched up the steps and into the house.

Once inside, Alex expected to be yelled at again, but all her mother said was, "Go upstairs and change your clothes and don't leave your wet clothes in your rooms. Put them in the bathroom."

Alex ran up the stairs ahead of Rudy. She didn't want to wait for him. She ran into her bedroom and flung the door shut. She quickly got out of her wet clothes, took them into the bathroom, and draped them over the tub. She then went back into her room and closed the door. She crawled up on her bed and stared out the window.

Still raining! But the sky didn't look quite so dark. *Maybe it will quit soon and I can check on my shoes. They've been out in that gutter in the rain all day.*

Alex was restless. She did a few somersaults on her bed, then jumped down and started pacing around her room.

"Why did it have to rain today? I could have bought new laces and got my shoes out of the gutter and everything. Brussels sprouts! The rain spoiled it all!" Alex was stomping around her room, now and then kicking at something. "I told Mom another lie in the car today (KICK!) and got in trouble for running out of the garage (KICK!) and all because of this stupid rain! It's (KICK!) all the rain's fault!" She gave her dresser an extra hard kick and hurt her foot. She fell to the floor and moaned, "Why is everything going wrong?"

"BANG! BANG! BANG!" Rudy opened her door and was shooting at her with his water pistol.

"Goblin!" shrieked Alex. "I'll teach you to open my door!" She jumped up and chased Rudy down the hall and into his room. She made a flying leap, tackled her brother, and sat on top of him. Rudy screamed. Alex had her fist in the air, ready to smash his face, when she heard her mother yell, "Children!" from the bottom of the stairs.

The way her mother yelled "Children!" reminded Alex of Mrs. Williams at choir practice Wednesday night. Mrs. Williams had also yelled "Children!" when Alex and Rudy had begun to fight. Now here she was again sitting on top of Rudy.

Mrs. Williams's words flashed through Alex's mind: Jesus didn't hurt the soldiers even though they were hurting Him.

Rudy wriggled and twisted underneath her. *Oh, brussels sprouts!* Alex thought angrily. *I know I'm not supposed to hit him back, but he's such a little brat!*

Several seconds went by. Alex slowly lowered her fist and through clenched teeth whispered, "Goblin, I'd love to clobber you, but I'm not gonna do it. I'm gonna be like the Lord was to the soldiers."

Rudy was too surprised to make any sound at all. He stopped his squirming and lay perfectly still.

Alex rolled off Rudy and collapsed on the floor. She was shaking. Alex thought that was the hardest thing she had ever done.

After a moment, Alex looked at her brother. Rudy was staring at her with wide-open eyes. Alex grinned. "You wanna do something in the playroom, Goblin?"

Rudy's eyes widened even more. He jumped up. "Yeah!" he shouted. He hopped to the doorway.

Alex started to follow but noticed a pile of wet clothes on the floor. "Oh, Rudy!" Alex said disgustedly. She gave her brother an annoyed look and carried the clothes to the bathroom where she hung them next to hers.

"You still gonna play with me?" Rudy asked anxiously.

Alex dried her hands on her jeans. "Come on, Goblin," she sighed.

CHAPTER 6

Fishing for Blue Jeans

"I'm gonna play with Alex!" Rudy joyously announced to Mother as he and Alex made their way to their own special room in the basement.

"That's nice!" answered Mother, looking pleased and surprised.

Alex smiled sweetly at her mother and followed Rudy down to the basement.

A large room filled with toys and not-so-good furniture awaited them. No one but Alex and Rudy used the playroom. Barbara had outgrown it, and their parents avoided it. "It's too dangerous for me," Father always said. "I might get hit by a speed skater or shot by a rocket." That was fine with Alex and Rudy. They loved having a room all to themselves. Alex had even tacked a sign on the wall that read, NO GRONUPS ALOWD.

"You wanna play race cars?" asked Rudy, scurrying around collecting cars from the speedway he had built with blocks.

"Yeah, maybe later," replied Alex. "First, let's warm up with 'jump the furniture.' "

"Okay!" agreed Rudy. This was a favorite game. They each took turns trying to go completely around the room without touching the floor. They had to jump from one piece of furniture to another. The first one to touch the floor was the loser.

Alex was crouched on the sofa ready to spring across to a chair when she noticed her mother passing through the other side of the basement carrying hers and Rudy's wet clothes. Pretty soon she could hear the hum of the washing machine. Mother went back upstairs.

Alex had leaped to the chair, then to the coffee table, over to the sofa, and was getting ready to jump onto the rocking horse when she remembered the three dollars she had left in the pocket of her jeans.

"Brussels sprouts!" she cried and ran to the washing machine.

"You lose!" Rudy shouted triumphantly.

Alex flung the lid of the washer open. All she could see was a swirling mass of soapy bubbles. She stared at the churning water trying to peer through the bubbles. Now and then she could see something dark whirling around. Could it be her blue jeans? It could, or it could be Rudy's or even something else Mom threw in with the load. She had to get her money!

Alex thought for a moment. *I could turn the washer off and get my jeans easily. No, that wouldn't work. I'm sure Mom would notice.* Mom always knew when the washing machine stopped even when no one else knew it was on!

"I won! I won! I won!" Rudy was hopping all around Alex. "Come on, Alex, let's play some more."

"Okay, Goblin, just give me a minute. Why don't you go build a really long race track so we can race our cars? I'll be over in a sec."

Rudy skipped back to the playroom.

I wonder if I can grab my jeans, thought Alex.

She started to reach her hand into the bubbles but then had a better idea. Mom kept long, skinny, round sticks down here somewhere. She used them for macrame. Aha! In a corner, Alex found a whole box of them. She picked out the longest one and carried it back to the washing machine.

Alex began fishing for her blue jeans. The first item she caught with her stick was Rudy's blue jeans. She draped them over the side of the machine. Next, she yanked out her father's old work shirt. She also caught her mother's apron, her own T-shirt, Rudy's flannel shirt, and Barbara's sweat shirt. As they came out, she hung them over the washer's side. But where were her jeans?

Alex stuck her pole in again. Yuck! All she caught was an old sock of Father's. She threw it back in. She climbed up on the washer and peered down into it. Maybe they were on the bottom? Alex jammed the stick way down into the machine. It stuck! She couldn't pull it out! She finally let go of it. The stick, standing straight up in the air, jerked back and forth.

"Funny, Alex! Funny!" laughed Rudy as he

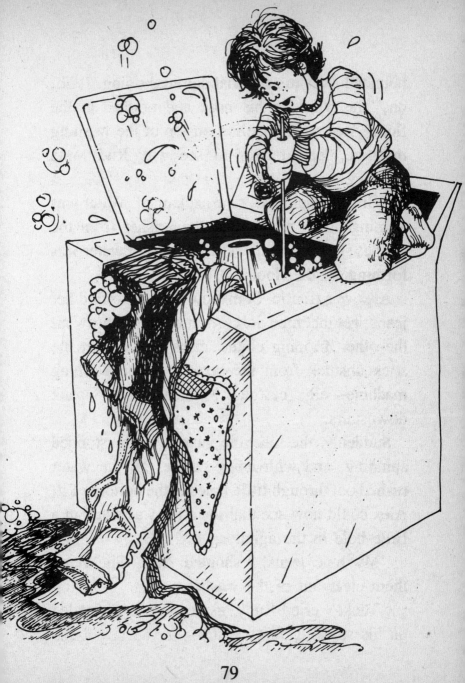

bounded over to see what she was doing. "Uh, oh," he wrinkled his nose and pointed at the floor. Alex, still kneeling on top of the washing machine, leaned over to see why Rudy was pointing.

"Brussels sprouts!" she exclaimed. Water was running down the side of the washer from the clothes she had piled over it. A pool of water was forming on the floor.

Alex was frantic. Somehow she had to find her jeans, get the three dollars out of them, throw all the other dripping clothes back in, and get the stick unstuck from the bottom of the washing machine—all before Mother came back downstairs.

Suddenly, the machine gave a lurch, stopped spinning, and with noisy gurgles all the water rushed out through little holes in the bottom of it. Alex could now see that the stick was stuck in a little hole in the agitator.

"My blue jeans!" shouted Alex. She flung them clear out of the washer.

"Yuck!" cried Rudy, as her wet jeans landed on his stocking feet.

Alex paid no attention to Rudy. She had to work fast. The washer was beginning to fill up with water again. At least it was clear water this time so she could see. Using all her strength, she twisted and jerked the stick until it finally came loose.

Alex leaped off the washing machine, threw the stick down with a clatter, and started shoving all the clothes back into the washer; all except her blue jeans. She grabbed them from the floor and searched her pockets. She found the three soaked dollar bills, then threw her jeans back in the washer and slammed the lid shut.

Still clutching the money, Alex found an old towel and dried the floor with it. She then dried the side of the washing machine. Satisfied that all was normal, Alex threw the wet towel in a corner where Mother wouldn't notice it right away. She unrolled the dollar bills and placed them in Miss Mushy's old dollhouse to dry. Nobody would find them there.

Alex walked over to where Rudy was putting the final touches on his race track. She sat down next to him. Her legs were trembling from all the nervous excitement. She hoped Mother wouldn't notice anything unusual about the washing machine. You never could tell about mothers. They always seemed to find out about the bad stuff kids did.

'*Specially my mom,* thought Alex. She remembered when she was younger, her mother saying, "Moms have eyes in the back of their heads." For a long time after that, Alex would stare at the back of her mother's head, half afraid of seeing an eyeball peeking out at her from under her mother's hair. Gross!

"Alex! Pick a car to race!"

"Huh? Oh, okay, Goblin. Let's race," answered Alex.

"Alex! Rudy! It's almost time for dinner. Come and wash up," Mother yelled from the top of the basement stairs.

Dinner? Alex was surprised. Had they been playing that long? She hurried up the stairs with Rudy close behind her.

Alex ran to the back door and looked outside. The rain had stopped, and the sun was shining.

She looked behind her. Mother was busy in the kitchen. Barbara was setting the table. Rudy was hopping between the kitchen and the dining room, getting in the way. She didn't see her father. Nobody was watching her. She opened the back door and darted outside. She ran to the rain gutter, expecting to find a pair of drenched tennis shoes.

Instead, the gutter was empty! She lay down on the wet ground and peered up the pipe as far as she could. No tennis shoes! Where were they? Where was the rock she'd stuffed in the pipe? Alex felt frantic again. She started looking all around the outside of the gutter pipe. There was the rock lying a few feet away! She was sure it was the same one. Could it have come loose? Could her shoes have been washed out of the gutter by the rain?

Alex made a quick search of the yard for her shoes. She didn't see them. *I don't think they could have been washed out of the pipe*, thought Alex. She remembered how hard she had to shove to get her shoes up the pipe in the first place. Still, it had been a really hard rain.

Alex carefully searched the whole backyard again. She looked under every bush and tree and along the fence and even on the other side of the fence, but no shoes. It was getting dark. Alex suddenly realized that she had been outside for a long time. Why hadn't anyone called her in for dinner? She was starving! She might as well give up. Her shoes had disappeared.

Alex stepped inside the house. No one was sitting at the dinner table. In fact, it looked as though her sister was carrying the last of the dinner dishes into the kitchen. Her mother was standing at the sink, putting dishes into the dishwasher.

They ate without me! Alex was surprised and a little angry. She'd never missed dinner before! She walked into the kitchen.

"Hi, Alex," said Barbara.

"Oh, hi, Alex," said Mother. She kept rinsing dishes as if nothing were wrong.

Alex didn't quite know what to say. Finally, she asked accusingly, "Did you guys eat dinner already?"

"Why, yes we did," Mother answered in a

cheerful voice.

"Well," Alex stamped her foot. "What am I supposed to eat?"

"Oh, that's right. You weren't here when everyone else was eating dinner," replied Mother. "Let's see. You could fix yourself a peanut butter sandwich."

Alex was shocked! A peanut butter sandwich for dinner? They hadn't even saved her a plate of food? She stared hard at her mother's back for a few angry seconds. Suddenly, tears began to fill Alex's eyes. Brussels sprouts! Nothing was right! Nothing was fair! She flew out of the kitchen and up to her bedroom in a rage.

Alex lay facedown on her bed clutching Garfield. Her tears soaked her pillow. She couldn't stop them from falling. Awful thoughts screamed inside her mind. *Nobody cares about me! Mom doesn't care if I'm hungry! She doesn't love me anymore!* Angry sobs shook her whole body. *Maybe I'll run away! They might be sorry then!* She cried and trembled for a long time.

Slowly—very slowly—Alex's anger turned to sadness. Her thoughts weren't screaming so

loudly now, but she was filled with terrible feelings. *Mom shouldn't love me. I lied to her! I'm a
horrible person! I feel all alone. No one under-
stands. Oh, somebody please help me! What
should I do?*

Alex was certain she had never been this miserable in her whole life. It was like lying at the
bottom of a huge pit with nothing but black walls
all around her. She couldn't get out of the pit. She
couldn't even move—she had no strength left.

It seemed as if she lay at the bottom of that pit
for hours. Wait! There was a light up there! Who
was making that light! All at once, Alex knew.
She lifted her hand up and tried to reach the light.
"Lord . . . Jesus," she whispered, "help me."

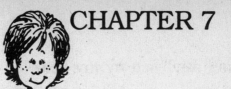

CHAPTER 7

The Lord's Answer

The first thing Alex saw when she opened her eyes the next morning was a peanut butter sandwich. She stared at it, rubbed the sleep out of her eyes, and stared at it again. A sandwich? Could the tooth fairy have made a mistake? No, no. The tooth fairy didn't bring peanut butter sandwiches! Just to be sure, Alex ran her tongue over her teeth. Nope, no new ones were missing. Oh, well, she was starving. Alex sat up, ripped the plastic wrapper off the sandwich, and ate it in four big bites.

"Good morning," said Mother from the doorway. She smiled at Alex when she saw the empty plastic wrap.

"Good morning," gulped Alex. She gave her mother a sticky smile. "Did you put a peanut butter sandwich by my bed?''

"Yes, I did,'' Mother replied. "I thought you might be extra hungry this morning. Now hop out of bed. Today is Friday,'' she added cheerfully.

That filled Alex with gloom. *Oh, yeah, Friday!* Alex used to love Fridays. In fact, she had even loved last Friday. Fridays meant ball practice and no more school until the next week. They meant Saturday was really close and Saturday's ball game. But this Friday would be awful. Brussels sprouts! She had to wear her boots again. Her coach would be furious. THE BULLDOZER would be mad, too. Another day of clomping and stomping. And what about the game tomorrow? A pitcher couldn't wear cowboy boots in a real game!

Alex dragged out of bed and got ready for school. She ate a second breakfast with her family. She didn't feel like joining in their morning chatter. She could think only of her problems.

At school, Alex had trouble concentrating. She worried and worried about ball practice and the game. *What will Mr. Glover do when I show up in cowboy boots again? He might not let me pitch. Maybe I'll skip practice. No, then he for sure won't let me pitch in the game. How did my tennis shoes disappear? What would my parents say if I told them I need another pair of shoes? What if I told them all that's happened . . . the whole truth?*

Brussels sprouts! I'd really get it for all the lies I've told! Maybe I could tell them that a mean kid stole my shoes. No, they'd want to know who he was and call his parents. . . . What if I told them a big dog grabbed my shoes and ran away? No, they wouldn't believe that. What should I do?

All day long these thoughts raced through Alex's mind. Whenever Mrs. Peppercorn asked her a question, Alex couldn't answer. Even at recess the thoughts wouldn't stop. All Alex did was sit on the ground and stare at her feet.

By the end of the day, Alex was exhausted from all her worrying. It hadn't helped a bit and now it was time for ball practice! She stumbled to the softball field in a panic. Never had her feet felt so heavy.

Alex reached the bench by the field. Her coach was busy talking to some teachers.

Maybe he won't notice me, hoped Alex. She yanked her mitt out of her backpack and started toward the pitcher's mound.

Jackie, the team's catcher, noticed her boots and yelled, "Are you crazy, Alex?"

"Clam up!" Alex shouted back. Brussels sprouts! It was just like Jackie to open her big mouth!

Alex drew her arm back, ready for her first warm-up pitch. As her arm began to swing forward, someone shouted, "ALEX!" She jumped. The ball dribbled out of her hand and rolled toward home plate. Slowly she turned and met the frowning eyes of her coach.

They stared at one another. Alex's legs quivered like Jell-O, her face felt hot, and her hands were sweating. Mr. Glover didn't seem to be in much better shape. His face was as red as Rudy's fire engine. His chest rose and fell with each angry breath. Alex thought she could almost see smoke rising out of the top of his head.

He didn't say a word. He just pointed his finger at her and then at the bench. Alex knew what he meant. She was benched! How devastating! The

team's star pitcher was benched! She hung her
head and, not looking at anyone, walked off the
field.

She heard her coach yell, "Sandy!"

"Brussels sprouts!" moaned Alex, "not Sandy
Anderson!" Sandy had been trying all spring to
take away Alex's number-one pitching spot. She
was a continual headache for Alex. Sandy was
constantly asking Mr. Glover if she could pitch
instead of Alex. Of course, the coach knew that
Alex was better. Still, Sandy was improving.

"Oh, brussels sprouts!" Alex sputtered.

"Tough luck," said a voice next to her.

Alex turned to see who it belonged to. Fat Lorraine! Alex felt even more depressed. Benched with Fat Lorraine! She was thoroughly humiliated. How was it possible that Alex, the best ballplayer, could be sitting next to Fat Lorraine, the worst ballplayer?

Fat Lorraine was smiling shyly at Alex. Then, as if she could guess what Alex was thinking, Fat Lorraine lost her smile and looked at the ground.

Alex turned her head away. She tried to concentrate on ball practice, but a funny thing kept happening. She kept thinking about Fat Lorraine!

Alex glanced quickly to her right. Fat Lorraine was chewing on her fingernails. She looked kind of sad. *It must be terrible to have to sit on this bench most of the time like Fat Lorraine does,* thought Alex. *I wonder if it hurts her feelings to be called "Fat Lorraine"? I wonder if she wishes that she was a good ballplayer?*

Alex was surprised at herself. She had never really paid attention to Fat Lorraine. *Oh, brussels sprouts, I have enough to worry about right now! I'm sitting here when I'm supposed to be out there in the field pitching!*

Alex watched Sandy throw a pitch. "Ball four!" yelled the coach disgustedly.

What am I going to do about tomorrow's game? Should I tell Mom and Dad about my shoelaces and my shoes? Alex wondered. She hunched over and held her head in her hands until practice was over.

"That's it for today! Tomorrow morning we play the Hornets! South Park field. Nine o'clock," Mr. Glover barked.

The bench rocked alarmingly as Fat Lorraine got up. Alex felt that she should say something nice to her.

"See you tomorrow," Alex said. It was all she could think of. Fat Lorraine's face brightened, and she waved good-bye to Alex.

Suddenly a hand gripped Alex's shoulder. She spun around. Her coach towered above her. "I cannot let you pitch tomorrow with those boots on," he growled. He looked at her, waiting for her to answer.

Alex didn't know what to say. Then to her horror, she felt tears spilling down her cheeks.

Choking back sobs, she grabbed up her backpack and started to run home.

When Alex reached her street she slowed down to a walk. She was out of breath, tired, and very miserable. She flopped down under a neighbor's tree and leaned back against its trunk.

How did things get so bad? Alex thought back to the beginning of her troubles. Jason and his dumb turtle had started everything! Brussels sprouts! She felt very sorry for herself.

After sitting awhile and remembering all that had happened to her in the last few days, Alex finally began to be honest with herself. *It's really the lies that are causing the trouble! I wonder how many lies I've told?* Alex began counting them.

Alex remembered telling her mother that Janie had borrowed her shoelaces. That had been the first lie.

The second lie was when she had told her mother that she'd left her backpack at school, when it was really under a bush.

Next, she had lied to her sister by saying she needed three dollars to buy a present for her mother. That was lie number three.

She'd also lied to her father when he had caught her coming in the back door so early yesterday morning. She had told him that she was checking the weather when she'd really been hiding her shoes in the gutter pipe. That was the fourth lie.

She had lied again to her mother in the car when she'd said that she and Janie were going to take a shortcut home in the rain when they had really been heading for the store. Lie number five!

Five lies! Five fingers were spread open on one hand. Alex was amazed. Had she really told five lies?

Tuesday was the day that Clementine got out of the fence and today was Friday. She counted the fingers on her other hand—Tuesday, Wednesday, Thursday, Friday—four days! Five lies in four days! "Plus a lot of other trouble," Alex grumbled. She'd made THE BULLDOZER, her coach, and the gym teacher mad by wearing her boots. She'd made her mother angry several times and had almost broken the washing ma-

chine and had missed dinner last night and . . . .
How could so much trouble start with one little
lie?

Alex laid her head on her knees and sighed,
"One lie seems always to lead to another lie. If I
go on like this, I'll be telling lies my whole life!"

Everything was all wrong. *There must be a way
to get rid of all this trouble and make everything
right again. But how?* wondered Alex.

She looked up and noticed the branches of the
tree above her. They were shaped like a great
umbrella hanging over her. Leaves were fluttering gently with little specks of sunlight flashing
through them. The sky was bright blue with
fluffy clouds. All at once, Alex knew who could
help her. If God could make the branches and the
leaves and the sun and the sky and the clouds,
then for sure He knew how to get a kid out of
trouble!

Right there, under that big tree in her neighbor's yard, Alex got to her knees. "Lord," she
prayed, "I've been messin' up. Please show me
what to do. Amen."

Almost immediately, a thought came to Alex's

mind. It was one that she didn't really like. She tried to push it away and forget it, but it wouldn't go away. No matter how hard she tried to think of something else, her mind kept returning to that one thought. After several minutes of hard thinking, Alex understood.

"I see what You're telling me, Lord," she said silently. "There's only one way out. I have to tell my parents the truth. I have to tell them everything that's happened. If I don't, then this mess will just get bigger."

Alex lay down on the grass and stared up at the sky. "It's gonna be hard to tell Mom and Dad. They'll probably scream and yell and have heart attacks and ground me for a whole year! But that's okay. I just gotta start doing what's right."

Alex was, once again, surprised at herself. She hadn't realized how much she needed to speak the truth. Now that she'd decided to tell the truth, another surprise came. She felt good! She felt happy!

There was, however, one more thing Alex needed to do. She got back on her knees to pray. "Lord Jesus, *help* me to tell Mom and Dad the whole truth. Amen.''

Alex felt so good that she skipped the rest of the way home. She wouldn't trade the peace she felt for anything—even if she did get grounded for a whole year!

CHAPTER 8

Alex Tells
the Truth

The house seemed empty as Alex, rather timidly, walked through the front hallway. Where was everybody? She had expected her mother to be busily fixing dinner, but the kitchen was empty. There was no sign of Rudy or Barbara. Her father wasn't in his chair reading the paper.

Alex crossed the dining room and then the living room. She turned a corner and stepped down into the family room. There were her parents sitting on the sofa. No one else was around. Alex had a strange feeling that they were waiting for her and that they already knew what she had to tell them.

"Hello, Alex," said her mother in a very quiet voice. "Please close the door."

"Firecracker," said her father, "we have something to talk over with you." He pointed Alex to a chair.

Alex closed the door but she did not sit down. She stood, facing her parents. *I just have to get this over with,* she thought.

"Wait a minute," Alex said. "Please, could I say something first?"

Her father looked surprised and maybe a little relieved. "Why, certainly," he answered gently, "go right ahead."

Alex hesitated. "Well," she finally said. "It's kind of a long something." Her voice sounded cracked and a little squeaky.

"We have all the time you need," Mother replied.

"Okay, uh, you see, well . . . it all started last Tuesday when Jason brought Clementine to school—you know, his turtle—and Clementine's a real fast turtle, and, well, she got outa the fence at recess and Jason was bawlin' and I just had to help get her back, and . . ."

With her heart pounding and her knees shaking, Alex poured out the whole story of the

last four days to Mother and Father. She talked very quickly, as if she couldn't get it out fast enough. While she was talking, Alex felt almost as if she were describing another girl's experiences. It hardly seemed real that all this had happened to her in such a short time.

Her parents never interrupted her story. Their nods and their understanding looks encouraged her to go on. When Alex described in detail the dog with the big teeth, her parents shuddered. When she told of her feelings of despair and guilt, their eyes filled with tears. They even laughed out loud when Alex told about the stick jerking around in the washing machine.

When Alex could think of nothing more to add, she flopped down on the sofa between her parents and looked from one to the other. She spread out her hands. "That's it," she said.

"Ahem," Father cleared his throat. "Well, Firecracker, that's quite a story. Tell me, what have you learned from all these experiences?"

Alex jumped up and then sat down on the floor in front of her parents.

"Oh, that's the neat part!" she exclaimed. "I learned that I was praying the wrong prayer!"

"Huh?" asked both her parents at once.

"Well, before tonight," Alex explained, "I kept asking the Lord to help me get my laces and my shoes back. See, I thought He should help me even though I kept on lying and getting in more trouble.

"But tonight," she continued, "I learned that what He really wanted me to do was to tell the truth. So, I prayed the right prayer. I asked the Lord to help me tell you the truth."

Alex paused and then added, "You know, the

shoes don't seem so important now. I guess what's important is telling the truth.'' She looked up at her parents.

"Alex,'' said her mother, "you have discovered the wonderful goodness of the Lord. He makes everything turn out for the best when we listen to Him and do what He says.'' Mother's eyes were shining with tears. "Oh, honey,'' she said, "you have made us so happy!'' She held out her arms and Alex rushed into them. Father wrapped his arms around both of them and all three held each other tight.

After several minutes, Alex wiggled. "Dad?'' she whispered.

"Hmmmm?''

"When I first came in here tonight, you said you wanted to talk over something with me,'' said Alex.

"Uh-huh,'' answered Father.

"Well, what is it?'' asked Alex.

"Ahem!'' Father cleared his throat again. He took out a handkerchief and blew his nose. Mother chuckled and grabbed a Kleenex and blew her own nose.

"Well, well, Firecracker, I'll just show you." Her father walked over to the desk, reached behind it, and pulled something out from underneath it.

Alex looked. It was a pair of tennis shoes. Her shoes. Only they didn't look much like her shoes. She examined them. The blue color was gone. Instead, they were ugly brown with dark streaks all over them. They were ripped and the entire heel of one shoe was torn out. They were so mangled that Alex couldn't tell which was the right or left shoe.

"Unbelievable!" gasped Alex, turning her shoes over and over in her hands.

"You are quite right," said her father. "It was unbelievable."

"But how did you get them?" exclaimed Alex. "I searched a long time in the backyard last night and never found 'em."

"I know that. I was watching you," Father replied.

Alex drew a breath in sharply. She stared at her father in amazement. He took the shoes from her and sat down.

"Let me explain, Firecracker," he said. "Yesterday, oh, about lunchtime, your mother called me at the office. She was frantic! She told me there was a huge waterfall flowing over our back door!"

"A waterfall?" interrupted Alex.

"That's what I said to her. 'A waterfall?' " answered Father. " 'Yes' she insisted, 'hurry up and come look at this.' " Father glanced at Mother and chuckled. "Well," he continued, "being the dutiful husband that I am, I raced home in the pouring rain to check out a waterfall."

"Oh, brother," sighed Mother.

Alex was impatient. Grown-ups always took so long to get to the point. "Was there a waterfall?" she asked.

"Indeed, a regular Niagara Falls poured over the back of our house," answered Father. He paused and looked at Alex.

"I stood in the backyard in the drenching rain with mud oozing into my shoes and studied the situation," stated Father. "As I stood there, I suddenly realized what might be causing this great catastrophe.''

"What?" shouted Alex.

Father leaned toward Alex and said in a low voice, "I thought there might be something clogging the gutter pipe!"

"Uh, oh," Alex mumbled.

"So, I investigated, and what did I find? One rock and two shoes crammed up the gutter pipe!"

"Brussels sprouts!" exclaimed Alex. She looked at her father. He didn't seem angry so she asked another question. "But how did that cause a waterfall?"

"Well, Firecracker, when the pipe's clogged up there's nowhere for the water to go, so it spills over the guttering at the top of the house," explained Father. "But what I want to know is how you got your shoes up there in the first place. It took me almost an hour to yank them loose!"

"It wasn't easy," Alex replied. She thought of her father out in that thunderstorm for a whole hour trying to pull her shoes out of the pipe. She looked at him with true remorse.

"I'm sorry, Dad," she apologized.

Alex looked at Mother. *Poor Mom. I've lied to*

her and made her angry and sad. I love them so much.

"I'm sorry, Mom," she offered.

"We know you are truly sorry, Alex," said her mother.

"And we forgive you," added her father. He reached over and patted her back.

Those were the sweetest words Alex had ever heard. She reached for their hands and held them tightly.

"You know something, Firecracker?" asked Father. "I think you were right when you said you prayed the right prayer. Just look what the Lord had me buy you this afternoon!"

He strode over to the desk and again pulled something out from underneath it. It was a box. He handed it to Alex.

Alex ripped the top off the box. She gave a cry of joy! Inside the box was a pair of brand-new *blue* tennis shoes!

"Oh, wow! Oh, wow! Brussels sprouts!" Alex danced around the room. Now she could pitch in tomorrow's game! No more sitting on the bench next to Fat Lorraine! Fat Lorraine? Oh . . . Alex stopped leaping. Her face became serious. "I learned something else today," she told her parents.

"What's that?" asked Mother.

"That some kids are lonely and sad because they're always getting their feelings hurt by other kids. Only the other kids really don't know how much they're hurting them." Alex told her parents how she felt sorry for Fat Lorraine.

"I never thought much about her before," Alex explained. "But at practice I couldn't stop thinking about her!"

"Hmmm, maybe that's the Lord working on you again," suggested Father.

Alex thought for a moment. "Maybe it's good that I had to sit on the bench today! The Lord's sure taught me a lot. And . . . maybe it's good, too, that I lost my laces . . . so that I could learn all this stuff."

Both her parents laughed.

"The Lord turns all things to good—if you obey Him," said Father.

"Well, I know two things for sure," Alex announced. "I'm not gonna lie anymore *and* I'm not gonna call Lorraine 'Fat' anymore!'' She sat down on the floor, yanked her boots off, and began to put on her new tennis shoes. ''Hey!'' yelled Alex, ''there's no laces in these shoes!''

Her new tennis shoes had Velcro straps instead. Alex had never had this kind before. She had always thought they were ugly. She looked up at her father.

''Sorry,'' he shrugged his shoulders, ''they were the only kind in your size.''

Alex stared at him for a moment, then grinned and said, ''Well, at least this way I can't lose my shoelaces! Wait a minute! If these were the only shoes in my size, I bet the Lord wanted me to have this kind so I'd be sure and not lose my laces again!''

All three of them looked at one another and burst into laughter. Alex was sure she could hear the Lord laughing with them.

''What's so funny?'' shrieked a small voice. Rudy had jumped into the room and was glaring at them. ''I'm starving!''

Just then Barbara came trotting around the corner and into the room. ''Sorry,'' she told her parents. "I kept him outside as long as I could."

"I know," said Mother, "and it's okay. We're all finished in here."

"How about pizza for everybody?" Father asked loudly.

Everyone shouted hooray and hurried to get ready to go out to eat.

Alex dashed down to the basement. She had just remembered something she had to do. She ran over to the dollhouse. The three dollar bills were still where she'd left them to dry the day before.

All of a sudden, an ugly thought passed through her mind. *You could keep them and tell Miss Mushy you lost them*. Alex was astonished! How could she even think about telling another lie?

"NO WAY!" she yelled out loud. Alex grabbed the money and ran upstairs.

She found Barbara in the bathroom combing her hair. "Here!" Alex pushed the dollar bills into her sister's hand. "I'm sorry," she said. "I lied to you! I didn't really want the three dollars to buy a present for Mom. I wanted it for something else.'' Alex then ran out the door to the car before Barbara could say a word. She didn't want to have to explain the whole thing to her, too.

Thank You, Jesus

Alex felt stuffed! She had just finished eating two pieces of pepperoni pizza, one piece of sausage pizza, and a half of a piece of canadian bacon pizza.

They were driving home from the restaurant. Father was listening to a baseball game on the radio. Mother was humming softly to herself. Alex was sitting between Rudy and Barbara in the backseat of the car. Rudy was strangely quiet.

Suddenly, Barbara cried, "Stop the car!"

"What?" yelled Father, slamming on the brakes.

"Oh, sorry, Dad, I didn't mean to startle you," answered Barbara quickly. "But would you stop at that shopping center coming up? Please, Dad, only for a minute? I need to get something. I can't tell you what," pleaded Barbara.

Father grumbled but turned the car into the parking lot and pulled into a nearby parking space. He turned and peered at his oldest daughter. "Will this spot do, your majesty?" he asked.

"Just perfect, Dad! Thanks," Barbara assured him. "Come on, Alex."

"Huh?" asked Alex.

"Come on! Hurry up, Alex!" cried Barbara, grinning at her sister.

"Me, too!" shouted Rudy.

"No! Not this time," said Barbara firmly. She pulled Alex out of the car and shut the door quickly.

Alex could hear Rudy's loud wailing as she followed her sister down a sidewalk. Barbara led her inside a small gift shop.

"What's going on?" Alex asked as they stepped through the door.

Barbara didn't answer. She walked over to a counter and motioned Alex to follow.

Brussels sprouts! Alex went over to see what Barbara was staring at.

"There. That's it!" Barbara cried. She pointed

to a tiny blue and white teapot on a shelf among other miniature items.

"That's what?" asked Alex. Miss Mushy was being so mysterious.

"That's the teapot Mom wants for her miniature collection," answered Barbara. "You know, to put in her printer's drawer!"

"Oh," responded Alex. She still didn't understand why Miss Mushy had to drag her in to see a teapot. She looked at Barbara and shrugged her shoulders.

Barbara started to explain, "Well, since tomorrow's Mom's birthday . . ."

"Oh, yeah," Alex interrupted. "Are you going to give that teapot to her?"

"No," replied Barbara, "you are!"

"Me?" Alex exclaimed in surprise. "I can't! I don't have any money." She looked at the price tag stuck on the bottom of the teapot. It read "$3.00."

"Remember the three dollars you gave back to me tonight?" her sister asked.

Alex nodded and looked at the floor. She didn't want to remember *that* three dollars.

"Well," Barbara continued, "I just happen to have it with me." She dug into her purse and held out the money to Alex. "Go on, take it," she urged Alex.

Alex saw the three dollar bills lying in her sister's hand.

"I can't pay you back for a while," said Alex, as she looked up at Barbara.

"I'm not worried about it," Barbara declared with a smile. "Here, you'll need a little extra for tax."

Alex whooped with joy and snatched up the

teapot and the money. She paid for it and then carried the bag carefully back to the car.

Alex and Barbara did not say a word as they climbed into the car. They could only giggle. All Father said was, "Very mysterious!"

Alex leaned against the backseat of the car and grinned. She was so happy! This had turned out to be a good day after all.

She glanced at Barbara. Her sister had done something really neat for her tonight! Maybe she wouldn't call her Miss Mushy so much anymore.

She looked at her parents in the front seat and remembered how loving and understanding they had been when she'd told them about all her lies.

She wiggled her feet in her new tennis shoes. They were bright and sparkling and felt so good on her feet. Tomorrow they would get all dirty at the ball game, but that was okay. Mom would wash them.

Alex thought about what her father had said earlier this evening—about the Lord turning all things to good. "You sure do, Lord," Alex whispered. "Thank You, Jesus, thank You for everything!"

Peanut Butter
and Jelly Secrets

Nancy Simpson Levene

Chariot Books™

CHAPTER 1

A Five-Dollar Mistake

"Mom! Janie says her mother can take us to the school carnival," Alex cried, dangling the telephone receiver by its cord.

"I want to go!" shouted a voice from the floor. Alex looked down. Her six-year-old brother, Rudy, was wrestling with their puppy, T-Bone.

"Now, Rudy, we have talked about this before," Mother said firmly. "You cannot go because you have had a bad cold this past week and I think you should stay home."

"It's not fair!" Rudy hollered and stomped from the room.

"Mom! Janie's waiting on the telephone. Can I go?" Alex danced around in a circle, twisting the telephone chord around her waist.

"Yes, I think that would be all right," answered her mother.

"YIPPEE!" Alex shouted. She started to tell Janie the good news, but she was so tangled in the telephone cord that she couldn't get the receiver up to her ear.

"Oh, Alex, for heaven's sake!" Mother laughed. She twisted and turned Alex around and around until Alex was free from the cord.

"I'm supposed to be at Janie's in fifteen minutes," Alex announced, hanging up the phone.

"Okay, Honey," her mother replied. "Comb your hair and have a good time."

"Mom, I don't need to comb my hair to have a good time."

"Comb it anyway, Alex," Mother laughed.

Alex grumbled but started upstairs to obey. She stopped suddenly. "Mom, I need money!" she shouted.

Mother hurried to the bottom of the stairs. "Alex, all I have is a ten-dollar bill. It's on top of my dresser. You can take it, but I want you only to spend half of it at the carnival. The other half is for your school lunch money next week. Do you understand?"

"Sure, Mom," Alex clattered up the rest of the steps.

"Alex!" called Mother. "Remember, five dollars is all you can spend."

"Brussels sprouts, Mom, I know what half of ten dollars is."

"I'm just making sure you understand," answered her mother.

Alex swooped a comb through her hair, jumped back down the stairs three steps at a time, and banged out the back door. She headed for the gate in the fence that separated her backyard from Janie's backyard.

Janie and Alex were best friends. Janie was not exactly like Alex and Alex was not exactly like Janie, but they were still best friends. Alex liked to climb things, like fences and trees and tall dirt piles. Janie would rather dress up in her mother's old clothes or bake a batch of cookies. Alex loved sports. She was on a softball team and a swimming team. Janie loved to dance. She took ballet and modern dance lessons. Yet, in spite of their differences, the girls loved to be with each other. They did things that they liked to do together—

like roller skating or bike riding or spending the night at each other's house. And sometimes Alex would play dress-up with Janie, and sometimes Janie would play softball with Alex.

"Alex! Are you ready?" Janie called from her back door. Alex ran the rest of the way to Janie's house and the two girls hopped in the car.

"Girls," said Janie's mother as they pulled into the school parking lot. "I will show you the booth in which I will be working. I want you to check in with me every hour so that I know you are all right."

"Okay," the girls agreed. They followed Janie's mother to her booth. It was called the Barrel Toss. Each child got three chances to throw a ball into a barrel. If the ball landed in the barrel, the child won a prize.

"Hey, I bet I can do this easy," cried Alex. She stood behind the line, swung her right arm in two circles, and let go of the ball. BAM! It plopped right into the barrel. So did ball two and ball three.

"Where's my prize?" Alex grinned.

Janie's mother laughed. "Alex, I don't think

we should let you play this game. You are too good. By the way, you have to give me a ticket before you can get a prize."

Alex ran to the ticket counter and bought a string of tickets. So did Janie. Alex gave one ticket to Janie's mother and received a pink bracelet as a prize. Janie's mother laughed at the disappointed look on Alex's face. She took back the bracelet and handed Alex a package with a ball and jacks inside.

"That's better," Alex told her.

"Okay, you two, scram, so I can set up my booth," ordered Janie's mother. "Have a good time and check in with me in an hour."

Alex and Janie scurried away. They stopped at a cotton candy stand and bought bright pink balls of the fluffy candy. Then they began their trip around the carnival, stopping to play the games that interested them.

Everywhere they went, they heard reports about the spooky haunted house set up in the basement.

"I don't think I want to go to the haunted house, Alex," said Janie after listening to someone tell about a gigantic mummy that greeted each visitor.

"Well," Alex replied. "I know my mom wouldn't want me to go. She doesn't even want us to watch scary movies."

The girls were standing in front of the Cake Walk room. "Let's try and win a cake," Janie suggested. She and Alex joined a group of people who were circling the room, stepping on numbers taped to the floor. Whenever the music stopped, a man called out a number. If someone was standing on the number he called, that person won a cake.

After three tries, Alex's number was called. She chose a chocolate cake with chocolate icing.

"Alex, that's neat!" Janie shouted. "Let's take it to my mom so she can keep it for you."

On the way back to the Barrel Toss, the girls spied two boys from their class.

"Uh, oh, Eddie Thompson and Allen Jacobs," whispered Alex. "Quick, don't let them see us."

But it was too late. "Whirlywind, where'd you steal that cake from?" Eddie hollered. He called Alex "Whirlywind" because of her fast pitching arm. Alex could pitch a softball better than any of the boys in her class.

"Better put that cake back," cried Allen in a loud voice. "You know it's not nice to steal!"

"She didn't steal it! She won it!" Janie shouted at the boys.

"Just go away," Alex told them. She kept on walking. Eddie and Allen were always causing trouble. She had learned that it was best to try and ignore them.

"Whirlywind, have you been to the haunted house yet?" called Eddie.

"Aw, I bet they are too scared to go," jeered Allen.

"We are not scared to go to the dumb old haunted house," Alex shouted at Eddie and Allen. "We just don't want to!"

"Chicken, chicken, chicken," the boys sang. They ran off making clucking noises.

"Oooooooh, they burn me up!" Janie stamped her foot.

After delivering the cake to Janie's mother, Alex surprised Janie by saying, "You know, maybe we really ought to try the haunted house."

"What?"

"Well, I was thinking. What if we are the only ones in our class that didn't go to the haunted house? I mean, everyone will think we were scaredy cats."

"Oh."

"Let's just go see what it's like," Alex urged. "We can leave if we want to."

"Okay," Janie said slowly. "I'll do it for you, but not for anybody else."

The girls ran down a hall to a stairway. At the top of the stairs was a sign that read, "THIS WAY TO THE HAUNTED HOUSE. ENTER AT YOUR OWN RISK."

"How much is it?" Alex asked a lady who was selling tickets.

"Fifty cents," the lady replied.

"Fifty cents! Alex, I only have a quarter left," Janie moaned.

Alex pulled her money out of her pocket. She had a five-dollar bill and three quarters. "My mom told me not to spend the five dollars, but with your quarter and my three quarters we can get in," she told Janie.

16

The girls handed the lady their quarters and followed the line of people down the stairs. About halfway down, the stairway disappeared. In its place was a giant slide. Alex peered down the slide. She could not see the bottom.

"I'll go first," she said bravely.

"Alex, I don't know about this," Janie whispered nervously.

"Janie, it'll be okay. We can go down together. Get on the slide behind me."

The two girls climbed onto the steep slide. They immediately plunged into a dark tunnel.

"Ahhhhhhh!" Janie screamed in Alex's ear.

Alex squinted through the darkness. She was suddenly filled with terror when she saw a ghostly form waiting for them at the bottom of the slide—the mummy!

Alex hardly ever screamed. But this time she did. It was hard to tell who screamed the loudest—Alex or Janie.

The girls hit bottom and landed on something soft and squishy. Alex could not keep her balance. She tried to stand up but fell back against Janie. The mummy bent over them. There were no eyes in its face, only dark holes where its eyes should have been. A loud horrible laugh came from deep in its throat.

Alex was terrified but somehow managed to pull herself to her feet. She grabbed Janie's arm and dragged her friend away from the mummy. The girls stumbled around a corner and BANG! They collided with a skeleton. Alex shrieked. Janie cried. Behind the skeleton, lying on the floor, was what looked like a dead body. Alex stared at it, fully expecting it to rise up and chase her. It did not move but the fear that it would move was awful.

Janie began sobbing hysterically. Alex moved herself and Janie slowly around the "body."

"RUN!" Alex cried.

Janie ran! She ran blindly, covering her face with her hands. Alex held onto Janie and steered them through the darkened maze. They raced past one horrible figure after another.

"GET OUT! GET OUT!" Alex's mind screamed. It was her only thought—to get out of there as fast as she could.

Finally, Alex glimpsed the EXIT sign. She

made for it but suddenly a ghost blocked the way. Alex, still clutching Janie, charged full speed into the ghost, knocking it back against a wall. "Ugh," came a muffled protest from the ghost. The girls ran through a doorway, up some stairs, down a hallway, and into the brightly lit gymnasium. They collapsed on the floor of the gym.

It was several minutes before either of them could speak. Then Alex announced, "I am never going into a haunted house again!"

Janie nodded. Her eyes were red from crying and her face was streaked with tears.

"I'm sorry, Janie, for taking you in there," Alex apologized.

"That's okay," Janie murmured. "At least now we can say we went to the haunted house," she added a little more brightly.

"Brussels sprouts," was all Alex replied.

"I'm thirsty," Janie said after a moment.

"Me, too," agreed Alex, "but we are out of money."

"Yeah," Janie sighed. "I wish we hadn't spent it on the haunted house. I'd like to try the Cake Walk again. Maybe I could win a cake this time."

Alex didn't say anything. She was thinking about the extra five dollars in her pocket—the money that her mother had told her not to spend. She was thinking about spending it anyway. After all, it was her fault that they were out of money. She had talked Janie into spending her last quarter on the haunted house. And her friend had been so scared. Maybe she could make it up to Janie by sharing the five dollars with her. Besides, what fun was a carnival without money?

"Aw, why not," Alex decided. She pulled the

five-dollar bill out of her pocket. "Let's get something to drink and eat. I'm starved."

Janie's eyes brightened. She followed Alex to the drink counter and then to the hot dog stand.

"I hope your mom doesn't get too mad when she finds out you spent the five dollars," Janie told Alex.

"Let's don't think about it now," replied Alex. "Come on, let's go to the Cake Walk."

CHAPTER 2

The Goblin Strikes

When Alex got home, her mother asked, "Did you have a good time at the carnival?"

"Sure," Alex answered, "it was great—except for the haunted house."

"The haunted house?"

"Yeah, I sorta talked Janie into going in it, and now I wish I hadn't."

"Was it pretty bad?" Mother asked.

"Really bad," Alex sighed. She told her mother about the mummy, the skeleton, the dead body, and the ghost that she knocked against the wall on the way out.

"Well, that's one way to get rid of a ghost," Mother chuckled.

"I don't understand it," Alex complained. "I didn't like the haunted house at all. Other kids liked it. Why didn't I?''

"Maybe it all seemed too real to you," Mother suggested.

"Yeah," Alex agreed. "Even though I knew they were only people dressed in costumes, they were really spooky."

Mother smiled. "I am sure I would have felt the same way. You see, Alex, I think that because we are Christians, we don't like to be around anything that seems evil—even pretend evil. The next time you feel scared, you might try saying a prayer. You will be surprised at how much that helps." Mother gave Alex a pat on the head, then looked at her face closely.

"I think you need to wash your hands and face. It looks like everything you ate at the carnival is still on your face. Did you save five dollars as I asked you to?"

Alex did not answer her mother because at that moment an arrow whizzed past her nose! It hit the refrigerator and stuck. Alex and Mother stared, openmouthed, at the arrow vibrating up and down on the side of the refrigerator. "Rudy!" they yelled.

A frightened face, smeared with bright-colored paint, peeked around the corner.

"Rudy! Come here this instant!" Mother demanded.

Alex watched her younger brother shuffle slowly into the kitchen. Rudy was not his real name. His real name was David, but he had called himself "Rudy" for as long as Alex could remember. Everyone called him "Rudy," except Alex. She usually called him "Goblin."

If her mother hadn't been so angry, Alex would have laughed out loud. Rudy's once blond hair was now streaked with blue, orange, green, and crimson color. It stuck straight up through a headband holding feathers that drooped to his chin. Globs of paint splotched his T-shirt and blue jeans. He clutched his bow and arrows behind his back.

"Rudy! I have told you many times not to shoot arrows in the house," cried Mother. "Don't you realize how dangerous it is to shoot arrows at people? Even the arrows with rubber tips? I don't ever want to see you do that again!"

Mother was furious. She took the bow and

arrows from Rudy and said, "You need to learn to obey your parents, Rudy. Right now I'm too angry to decide your punishment. I want you to go upstairs. You'll have to take a bath and wash your hair. What is that stuff in your hair and on your face?"

Rudy hesitated, but finally said in a low voice, "Barbara's paint."

"Uh, oh!" Alex gasped. Their older sister, Barbara, was drawing a world map for a special school project. She had been working on it for two weeks.

"Barbara's poster paint?" Mother exclaimed. A horrified look crossed Mother's face. She grabbed Rudy by the arm and marched upstairs to Barbara's bedroom. Alex followed. There, on a desk, was the almost finished poster. Drops of fresh paint were now splattered over one corner of the map. To Alex it looked as if the sky above Alaska had multicolored chicken pox.

"You are in double trouble!" Mother told Rudy. She swatted his bottom. Rudy howled his way to his bedroom.

Alex tiptoed to her own bedroom. It was best to stay out of the way of an angry mother. She was glad that it was her brother who was in trouble and not herself. She hadn't done anything wrong. Or had she? Hadn't she just spent five dollars at the carnival that she wasn't supposed to have spent? Brussels sprouts! She had disobeyed her mother, too!

"Better not tell Mom about the money right now," she told herself. "Better wait until she's in a good mood."

Alex stayed in her room until almost dinnertime. She heard her sister scream when the ruined map was discovered.

"You could always make those colors into a rainbow," suggested Alex as she entered Barbara's bedroom. "It'd be sort of pretty to have a rainbow over Alaska."

Her sister didn't answer. She just stood over the map and glared at it. Alex left the room. "I guess Miss Mushy doesn't want to talk about rainbows right now," Alex decided.

Alex called her sister "Miss Mushy" because her sister liked to dress up in pretty dresses, curl her hair into different styles, sunbathe for hours in the hot sun, and paint her fingernails different shades of color—all things that Alex thought were dumb or boring.

"Oh, well," Alex told herself. "Miss Mushy probably wouldn't like the rainbow idea anyway. She never likes my ideas. Just because she's almost thirteen and I'm only nine, she thinks I'm a dumb little kid!"

That evening at dinner, when Alex's father asked her about the carnival, Alex quickly changed the subject. She did not want to talk about it because she did not want her mother to

27

remember the five dollars she was supposed to have saved for lunch money. No one asked her about the haunted house. Her family's thoughts turned to Barbara's poster.

"What can I do?" Barbara wailed. "I have to turn in the map to my teacher on Tuesday. I can't possibly do it all over again. It took me a week to draw and another week to label all the countries and cities and rivers and oceans!" She hid her face in her hands.

"You're right," agreed Father. "Tomorrow's Sunday. That doesn't give you much time." He reached over and patted Barbara's arm.

"There must be something you can do to fix it," said Mother.

"It's ruined!" Barbara moaned. "Ruined!" She slapped the table with her hand and glared at Rudy. "It's all your fault!"

Rudy stared at his toes and didn't answer.

"Maybe you could cover up the splotchy part with white paint and then draw in the top part of Alaska again," suggested Mother.

"I couldn't get it to match," complained Barbara. "My teacher would think that I goofed!"

"I told her she ought to make it into a rainbow," Alex told her parents.

"A rainbow?" smiled Mother.

"Oh, brother," Barbara scowled.

"Wait a minute! That's it!" shouted Father.

"It is?" asked Alex, Mother, and Barbara.

"Sure! You've heard of the northern lights over Alaska, haven't you?" Father asked them.

"What's that got to do with a rainbow?" Barbara frowned.

"Nothing, really," Father admitted. "The rainbow idea made me think of them." He smiled at his older daughter. "I think you might be able to turn the paint drops into beautiful northern lights. After all, you are the artist of the family."

"Hmmm" considered Barbara. The frown slowly left her face as she thought more and more about the idea.

Father glanced at Alex with a twinkle in his eye. Alex was thrilled to think that one of her ideas might help to solve an important problem. They watched Barbara's face anxiously.

"What color are the northern lights?" Barbara asked her father.

"I think they're a greenish color," he replied.

"I thought they were pink or red," Mother disagreed.

"I'm not sure," reflected Father. He turned to Barbara. "You'll have to look them up in the encyclopedia."

The next day, Barbara worked on her map. She informed her parents that they were both right about the color of the northern lights. The encyclopedia said that they were usually green, but when the lights were especially strong, they had a reddish color.

Alex paid no further attention to the map. She and Janie were busy designing a playhouse. They hoped their fathers would build it for them. Rudy was grounded. Mother said she was the one who was really being punished, because she was stuck inside with Rudy all day.

On Monday morning, Alex's mother reminded her to take her lunch money to school. She didn't ask Alex if she had the money. She just reminded her to take it.

While walking to school with Janie, Alex felt uneasy. She hadn't said that she had her lunch money—so she hadn't actually told her mother a lie. Still, by not answering her mother, Alex had let her mother think that she had her lunch money.

"Brussels sprouts!" Alex yelled out loud.

Janie jumped at the outburst. "What's the matter?" she asked Alex.

"Oh, I'm just getting mixed up," sighed Alex. "I mean, I guess I should tell Mom about us spending all that money at the carnival, except then I'll get in trouble."

"I forgot all about that!" Janie exclaimed. "You mean you haven't told your mom yet?"

"No," Alex sighed.

"Alex?" Janie suddenly stopped and stared at her friend. "Does that mean you don't have any lunch money today?"

"Yep."

"What are you going to do at lunchtime?"

Alex shrugged her shoulders. "Just not eat, I guess."

"But, Alex, you have to eat lunch!" Janie cried. "They don't just let kids sit in the cafeteria and not eat anything. Mrs. Tuttle would be worried and call your mom or something!''

Alex's eyes opened wider and wider as she slowly realized that Janie was right. Her teacher would not let her go without eating lunch. What was she going to do?''

''I'll have to hide somewhere,'' decided Alex.

''What?'' Janie shouted. ''Alex, where could you hide?''

''I don't know but I'll think of someplace,'' Alex answered.

''I don't think it's going to work, Alex,'' Janie warned. ''I think you're going to get in trouble!''

All morning long, Alex worried about lunchtime. What was she going to do? Where could she hide? She couldn't stay behind in the classroom. Mrs. Tuttle surely would notice if she didn't line up and follow everybody down the hall. What could she do?

By the time Mrs. Tuttle called everyone to line up for their march to the cafeteria, Alex still had not thought of a good hiding place. She let everyone else get in line and then she shuffled to the end of it. Her heart was pounding. She knew she had to find somewhere to hide before she reached the cafeteria.

As the class moved down the hallway, Alex lagged further and further behind. She frantically considered every door she passed. *The library? No, the librarian would see me. The nurse's office? No, I'd have to say I was sick, and she'd call my mom. Hey! Wait a minute! I know!*

Quick as a wink, Alex opened a door, stepped inside, and closed it as quietly as she could. She leaned against the closed door and waited until she could no longer hear footsteps. Finally, the only thing she could hear was her own rapid breathing and thumping heart.

Alex sank to the floor. "Now, I've really done it," she told herself. "If Mrs. Tuttle catches me in the janitor's closet, I've had it! Brussels sprouts!"

CHAPTER 3

A Dark Hideout

It was dark in the janitor's closet—so dark that all Alex could see were tiny cracks of light around the door edges. She sat on the floor, her back against the door, staring into the blackness of the closet.

"Don't be scared!" she whispered to herself. "There's nothing in here 'cept a bunch of rags and mops and brooms and stuff like that."

Still, it was awfully dark, and Alex kept thinking about the haunted house with its terrifying mummy, skeleton, dead body, and ghost. But she also remembered her mother's suggestion to say a prayer whenever she was afraid. "I'll say something from the Bible," Alex decided.

She thought of all the Bible verses she knew. She couldn't remember any about being shut in a dark closet. There was, of course, the 23rd Psalm. Alex had memorized it when she was only five years old. She knew it was a good psalm to say whenever she was afraid or in trouble, but there was a particular part of that psalm that frightened her. It was the part about walking "through the valley of the shadow of death." Many times she had tried to imagine what the valley of the shadow of death might be. She shivered every time she thought about it.

But Alex could think of no other Bible verse to say. She took a deep breath and recited Psalm 23 in a loud whisper:

The Lord is my shepherd; I shall not want. He maketh me to lie down in green pastures: he leadeth me beside the still waters. He restoreth my soul: he leadeth me in the paths of righteousness for his name's sake. Yea, though I walk through the valley of the shadow of death, I will fear no evil: for thou art with me; thy rod and thy staff they comfort me. Thou preparest a table before me in the presence of mine enemies:

thou anointest my head with oil; my cup
runneth over. Surely goodness and mer-
cy shall follow me all the days of my life:
and I will dwell in the house of the Lord
for ever.

Alex sighed. Even though she didn't understand it, the psalm had made her feel better.

Suddenly a loud ringing noise shattered the
silence of the closet. Alex jumped to her feet. For
a moment she thought the whole closet might
explode from the sound! What was it?

After a few seconds, Alex realized that that
noise was the same school bell that rang many
times during a day. Somehow it sounded different and a lot louder from inside the janitor's
closet. That ring meant that the third and fourth
graders' lunch period was over and it was time
for recess. Alex wondered how she was going to
be able to get back in line with her classmates
without Mrs. Tuttle seeing her.

She opened the door of the closet a tiny crack—
just enough to peek out into the hallway. She
could hear footsteps—many footsteps—coming
her way.

Children and teachers began to pass by her door. Suddenly, Alex saw Janie. She longed to cry out to her friend but she didn't dare.

All of a sudden, a figure blocked the crack through which Alex was peeking. Mrs. Tuttle! Alex didn't breathe. Her hand on the doorknob shook so much that she was afraid it might rattle the door!

Mrs. Tuttle stood in front of the janitor's closet for several seconds. Why had her teacher stopped? Had Mrs. Tuttle somehow seen her?

Her teacher motioned for the children in line to hurry up. She then continued to lead them down the hall. Alex watched her classmates, one by one, pass by the crack.

Alex let out a big gasp of air. That was close! Now came the hard part. Somehow, she had to get to the end of the line without anyone seeing her. She would wait until the last child in line passed her and then she would sneak behind that person. She had to be quick!

Soon, Alex saw her chance and sneaked rapidly out of the closet. She began to march right behind Lorraine, the last person in line.

Alex's blood pounded in her head. She felt hot and shaky, but she kept marching. Lorraine gave Alex several surprised and confused backward glances.

The line of children moved through the outside doors and onto the playground. As Alex passed Mrs. Tuttle at the door, she was almost sure that her teacher looked at her in a funny way.

Alex kept marching out the door and all the way to the far fence of the playground. She noticed Janie and several other friends following her, but she didn't stop until she reached the fence. Only then did she feel she could breathe again.

"ALEX!" Janie ran up to her friend. "You weren't at lunch! Did you hide somewhere?" Janie looked almost as worried as Alex felt. Alex quickly told her and the other girls about her adventure in the janitor's closet.

"Here," Janie dug in her pocket, "I saved you some crackers. It was all I could get."

Alex took the package of crumbled crackers from Janie and smiled. It was just like Janie to think of her friend being hungry. Alex was so

grateful and so glad to see her friend again that she did something unusual. She gave Janie a great big hug!

When Alex got home from school, she had a headache. She hardly ever got headaches—just when she was sick. She also felt tired and dizzy. She was sure it was from skipping lunch. All she'd had to eat since breakfast was a package of crackers. The thought of missing all of her lunches this week was awful. What could she do? Alex was too hungry to think. Would dinner never come?

Suddenly a joyful shout came from her sister's bedroom. Alex ran across the hall and into Barbara's room.

"HURRAY! I JUST FINISHED IT!" Barbara cried. "Well, what do you think?" she asked Alex, holding her world map up for Alex to see.

"Brussels sprouts," gasped Alex. She could no longer see the multicolored chicken pox that had been there before. In its place a greenish glow appeared. Above the glow, brilliant green bands of color arched across the sky over Alaska and Canada. Beams of light shot upward through the bands toward the middle of the sky.

The longer Alex stared at the map, the more the beams seemed to flash and sparkle, almost as if they were moving. How had Miss Mushy done it?

"Amazing!" whispered Alex. She turned to her sister. "Mom's right. You should be an artist when you grow up."

"Think so?" grinned Barbara. "I think it turned out pretty good, myself." She put an arm across Alex's shoulder. "Thanks for the idea, Squirt."

Just then Mother called, "DINNER!"

"Finally!" Alex shouted. She raced downstairs to the dining room and was the first to plop into a chair.

Alex ate everything on her plate and asked for more. She didn't even complain about eating coleslaw.

"Well, Firecracker," her father commented after her second helping, "it looks like you have a bottomless pit!" Father was always cracking goofy jokes. He called Alex "Firecracker." He had nicknames for Barbara and Rudy, too. He called Barbara "Princess" and Rudy "Steamroller."

Alex grinned at her father. She was feeling much better now. She grabbed a drumstick off the chicken platter and announced, "One more piece for the pit!"

Her mother rolled her eyes at Alex. "Didn't you eat very much at lunch today, Alex?" she asked.

"Lunch!" Barbara interrupted. "I almost forgot! I need to take a sack lunch tomorrow. We're going on a field trip."

As the rest of the family discussed Barbara's field trip, an idea came to Alex. "That's it!" she told herself. "I can take a lunch to school tomorrow, and I won't have to sit in the janitor's closet. I'll have to be real sneaky and make it when nobody's looking since Mom doesn't like us to take our lunches. She thinks we get better stuff to eat at school—like yucky vegetables."

After dinner, Alex waited for Mother to finish cleaning in the kitchen. But as soon as Mother left the kitchen, Barbara began making her lunch to take on the field trip. By the time her sister was finished, it was time for Alex to get ready for bed. She still hadn't been able to make a lunch for tomorrow.

"Oh, well, guess it's the janitor's closet again," Alex sighed. As she got into bed, her eyes caught sight of her clock radio sitting on a table by the bed. She could set her alarm for the middle of the night and, while everyone else was asleep, make a secret lunch!

Alex sat up in bed and reached for her clock radio. She held down the button that changed the alarm. It was fun to watch the numbers whiz by. When the numbers said *12,* she let up on the button. That would be midnight! Surely her family would all be asleep at midnight.

Alex lay down again. It was exciting to think of a secret journey at midnight. Alex had a hard time going to sleep. When she finally did fall asleep, she had the strangest dream. She was running through a beautiful green meadow when suddenly Mrs. Tuttle popped out from behind a rock and told her to get in line. She tried and tried to find the end of the line, but every time she thought she'd found it, another child would appear. There seemed to be no end to the children and no end to the line! A noisy school bell kept ringing through her dream. It hurt her ears.

Suddenly, Alex awoke. That wasn't a school bell. That was her alarm. It was midnight!

CHAPTER 4

Midnight Sneak

Alex fumbled for her radio and shut off the alarm. Her ears continued to ring from the noise. Her bleary eyes squinted at the clock. Midnight!

She sat still for a long time and listened. She had to be sure that no one else had been awakened by the alarm. She could hear nothing from the other bedrooms except her father's snoring.

Alex silently crept to the top of the stairs and looked down. The first few steps were softly lit by the hallway night-light, but the bottom part of the stairs was pitch black!

"You have to go down there," Alex told herself. "You can turn on a light when you get downstairs." Forcing herself to be brave, Alex sneaked down one step at a time. "Brussels

45

sprouts, these steps are squeaky." Funny, she didn't remember them being so squeaky in the daytime. With every squeak, Alex stopped, afraid that her parents might hear her. "Shhhhh!" she whispered to each step.

When she was almost to the bottom, Alex peered over the railing. Dim light from outside shone through the living room windows, casting eerie shadows all over the room. Alex took a deep breath, hurried down the rest of the steps, ran to the nearest lamp, and switched it on. Instantly, the shadows disappeared.

Snapping on lights as she went, Alex rushed to the kitchen. She jerked an apple and the grape jelly jar from the refrigerator. She dug the bread out of the bread box and grabbed the peanut butter off a shelf. Working furiously, Alex slapped together two peanut butter and jelly sandwiches and fitted them into sandwich bags. She quickly rinsed off the apple and dried it. She dumped all of it into a paper sack, trying not to let the bag rustle too loudly.

As she worked, Alex kept glancing over her shoulder, half expecting to see someone watch-

ing her. She felt like a burgler in her own house!

After dropping a handful of cookies into the sack, Alex carried it carefully over to her backpack which was hanging on a hook by the front door. She stuffed her lunch inside her pack, wincing at every rattle it made.

"Whew," Alex sighed, "that's done." Now all she had to do was turn off the lights and go back upstairs to bed. She returned to the kitchen and flipped the light switch. Immediately, the kitchen was filled with shadows. Alex hurried through the dining room and switched off the light. Entering the living room, she stopped by the lighted lamp. This was the hardest light of all to turn off because as soon as she did the entire house would plunge into darkness.

It's amazing how one light can make you feel so safe, she thought as she stood by the lamp. *I know that when I turn off this lamp, I'll still be in my living room but it won't feel like my living room because it'll be dark and spooky. I wish I had a lamp I could carry around all the time. Then I wouldn't be afraid of dark houses or dark janitor's closets.*

Alex moved so that she was as close to the stairway as possible but still able to reach the lamp. She tried to measure with her eyes how many steps she'd have to take to go from the lamp to the stairs. She then quickly switched off the lamp.

After stumbling to the dark stairway, Alex climbed rapidly. She didn't bother about squeaky steps this time. All she cared about was getting to her bedroom as fast as she could.

When she reached the top of the stairs, she scurried into her room and leaped on her bed.

Brussels sprouts! She had done it!

Morning came too quickly for Alex. It seemed that she had just fallen asleep again when she felt someone pulling at her arm.

"Alex! Wake up! Your alarm didn't go off this morning and it's late." Her mother's voice cut through the dark blanket of sleep.

Alex tried opening her eyes. They didn't want to open. The sunlight from the window was too bright. She squinted at Mother.

"Alex, Honey, you need to get up and get going," her mother told her. "I thought you were already up or I would have come in here sooner. You must have forgotten to set your alarm. Come on, hop out of bed."

Alex did not exactly "hop" out of bed. She kind of rolled, slid, and fell out of bed.

"Get some clothes on and run downstairs," ordered Mother. "Your breakfast is already on the table."

When Alex got downstairs she found bacon and eggs waiting for her on the kitchen table. Her mother and sister were standing in the kitchen. Mother was pointing at the kitchen counter and staring at her sister. Barbara, with her hands on her hips, was staring back at Mother.

"Barbara, you must have forgotten to clean up the counter after you made your lunch last night," accused Mother.

"Mom, I told you. I remember wiping the counter after I made my lunch," insisted Barbara.

"Well, you certainly didn't do a very good job. There are crumbs all over, and look at this knife. It's stuck to the counter with peanut butter!"

"I did make a peanut butter sandwich," Barbara admitted, "but I'm sure I didn't leave the knife stuck to the counter."

"If you didn't, then who did?" asked Mother. "Nobody else made a peanut butter sandwich last night."

Alex choked on her eggs. She was the one who had left the knife stuck to the counter after making her sandwich last night. Now, Miss Mushy was getting the blame. She guiltily watched as Barbara shrugged her shoulders and began cleaning the knife and wiping the crumbs and clumps of peanut butter and jelly off the top of the counter.

As they walked to school together, Alex told Janie how she had sneaked downstairs and made her lunch at midnight.

"Wow, Alex, weren't you scared?" Janie asked.

"Yeah, some," Alex admitted. She kicked a rock, sending it flying down the hill. "You know, Janie, I've been thinking. I've been doing some pretty bad things, like hiding in the janitor's closet and making lunch in the middle of the night, and . . . well, none of it would have happened if we hadn't spent the extra five dollars at the carnival."

"Yeah," Janie agreed.

"I wish we hadn't spent it," sighed Alex.

"Me, too," said Janie.

When Alex's class lined up for its usual lunchtime march to the cafeteria, Alex happily clutched her sack lunch. No janitor's closet today, she sighed in relief. There was one thing she'd forgotten—milk money. Oh, well, she'd have to do without a drink.

When Alex entered the noisy cafeteria, she

hurried to a seat beside Janie. "Boy, am I glad you brought your lunch today, Alex," exclaimed Janie. "I'd hate to think of you spending two days in a row inside that—"

"Shhhhh!" Alex clapped her hand over her friend's mouth. She frowned at Janie and then motioned toward some boys who had sat down at the end of their table. Eddie Thompson was one of them. If Eddie heard about Alex hiding in the janitor's closet, he'd tell Mrs. Tuttle just to get Alex in trouble. He was already angry with Alex for getting the largest and fastest hermit crab in the class. Could she help it if she'd drawn its number out of Mrs. Tuttle's hat the day they were making terrariums?

"Mmmmhhppff!" mumbled Janie. She was trying to remind Alex to take her hand off her mouth. The girls around them giggled. Alex quickly lowered her hand.

"Did you have to do that, Alex?" complained Janie.

"I didn't want the boys to hear you," Alex explained. "We all have to be careful and not let anybody know what I did yesterday or I'll be in big trouble," she told all the girls at the table.

The girls agreed to keep their secret and soon were talking and laughing about other matters. Alex found a way to eat her lunch without getting too thirsty. She would eat a bite of apple after every bite of peanut butter sandwich. That way the juicy apple kept her teeth from sticking together.

"Ouch!" Alex cried suddenly. Something had hit her on the nose! Whatever it was bounced onto the table. Alex peered at what looked like a mushy grape.

"HEY! HOW 'BOUT ANOTHER EYE-BALL?" Sinister laughter exploded from the boys' end of the table. Another round object was flipped from a spoon. It hurtled through the air and splashed into Janie's soup.

"YEEACK!" screeched Janie as drops of to-mato soup splattered all over her white blouse.

"CUT THAT OUT, EDDIE THOMPSON!" shouted Alex. She quickly ducked under the table as she saw several boys loading their spoons.

SMACK! SPLAT! SMACK! SPLAT! SMACK! SPLAT!

"EEEEEK!" the girls screamed. They all quickly joined Alex under the table as a shower of "eyeballs" splashed around them.

"EYEBALLS! FROGS' EYEBALLS!" roared the boys.

"CHILDREN! WHAT'S GOING ON HERE?" a voice cut through the uproar. They all knew that voice—Mrs. Tuttle.

Upon hearing her teacher's voice, Alex crawled out from under the table. Her foot squished something soft. She jumped back. "Don't be ridiculous," she told herself. "Those aren't eyeballs. They're only grapes." Just the same, Alex was careful where she put her feet.

"You boys will use your recess to clean up this mess!" ordered Mrs. Tuttle. "Girls, pick up the rest of your lunches and move to a clean table."

The girls hurried to obey. The table was a disaster. Smashed grapes covered it. Some of the drinks and soup had been spilled when the girls had scrambled under the table.

Mrs. Tuttle sat down beside Eddie. Alex stole a peek at the boys. They were staring at their plates and looking miserable.

As soon as Alex and her friends were settled at another table, they began to giggle. Those boys! Wouldn't they ever learn to behave? The girls happily finished their lunches and skipped out to the playground for recess.

CHAPTER 5

Treasure Hunting

That evening after dinner, Father, Mother, Barbara, Alex, and Rudy gathered in the family room. It was Tuesday, and every Tuesday evening the family joined together for what they called Treasure Hunting. Father or Mother would read a story from the Bible and then talk about it. As the family discussed the story, they would discover God's messages in the story. Those messages were the treasure. They would see how the treasure could help them in their own lives.

Alex loved Treasure Hunting. The stories were fascinating, and it amazed her to think that they were true. "Things must have been a lot more exciting back then," she told herself. "Today nobody gets thrown into a lions' den like Daniel

or lives inside a whale like Jonah or kills a giant with a slingshot like David. Brussels sprouts! We don't even have any giants around here!''

As much as Alex liked to hear the Bible stories, she liked even more having her family close around her. It reminded her that her family would always be available whenever she needed them. She could feel God's love surrounding and protecting them all.

''All righty, buccaneers, hoist the sail! Raise the anchor! Climb the crow's nest! We're off to search for treasure!'' Father's eyes rolled as he twirled the ends of an imaginary mustache. On his head was a magnificent sea captain's hat, a bright red plume stuck in its band. Mother had made the hat for him several years ago when he had dressed as Christopher Columbus for a costume party.

Seeing Father in that hat always made Alex and Rudy giggle. "Look alive or you'll be swabbing the deck!" he told them.

"What are we going to read tonight?" Barbara asked.

"We're not going to read anything tonight," Father announced. He held up his hands as the children began to protest. "I'm going to ask you a question. I want to see if you can answer the question by remembering the stories we already have read."

"What's the question?" Alex immediately wanted to know.

"I was just getting to that, Firecracker. Can you remember any Bible stories in which a person obeyed God?"

"Easy!" cried Alex. "How 'bout Moses?"

"Good. Tell us how Moses obeyed God."

"Are you kidding?" Alex exclaimed. "There were lots of ways he obeyed God. He went to Egypt and told Pharaoh to let the Israelites go; he had all the Israelites put blood over their doors so the Angel of Death would pass over their houses; and he stretched his staff over the sea so that the sea opened up. God told him to do all that stuff."

"That's right, Firecracker! I'm glad to see you've been paying attention to my reading," teased Father.

"Oh, Dad," Alex sighed.

"Would you say that good things happened because Moses obeyed God?" Father asked Alex.

"Sure," she answered. "The Israelites got away from Pharaoh and didn't have to be slaves anymore."

"Very good," her father praised her. "Who else can think of someone who obeyed God?"

"I can," Barbara said. "Shadrach, Meshach, and Abednego obeyed God's commandment not to worship any idols. When King Nebuchadnezzar asked them to worship a gold statue, they wouldn't do it."

"Right," Father agreed, "and what happened to them?"

"Well, they did get thrown into a furnace, but God protected them. When they came out without any burns, the king saw how powerful God was, and no one had to worship the gold statue anymore."

All the time that Barbara was speaking, Rudy bounced up and down on the sofa, his eyes sparkling. As soon as she finished, he popped up from his seat.

"I know one! I know one!" he cried.

"Who?" Father asked him.

"Noah," Rudy proudly announced.

"How did Noah obey God?" asked Father.

"He built the ark when God told him to," Rudy told him.

"And what happened after he built the ark?"

"Well, a big flood came and drowned all the people except Noah and his family and the animals," answered Rudy.

"Very good, Steamroller," Father winked at Rudy. "You've all thought of good examples and we've seen good things happen when people obey God. Now . . ."

"Wait a minute," Mother interrupted. "Don't I get a turn?"

"Oh, of course. Excuse me," replied Father. He made a low bow to Mother. They all laughed.

"I'm thinking of Jesus," said Mother. "He obeyed God and died on the cross for us so that God would forgive our sins and give us eternal life."

"Right. I'm certainly glad Jesus obeyed God," Father exclaimed.

"Me, too," cried Alex. "Now we can live forever with Him." Everybody nodded their heads in agreement.

"I have another question for you," said Father. "Who can think of someone who didn't obey God?"

"Oh, I know," Barbara exclaimed. "Adam and Eve."

Father looked at Barbara. "What happened because Adam and Eve did not obey God?"

"Very funny, Dad," replied Barbara. "We all know what happened in that story. You know, evil came into the world, and that's why the world's in such a big mess now."

"I have to agree with that," said Father. "Adam and Eve listened to Satan instead of to God. They ate an apple that God told them not to eat. They disobeyed God. Did you know that to disobey God is a sin? Look what happened to the world when Adam and Eve disobeyed.

"Yes, Firecracker? I can see you're bursting to tell us about someone else," Father chuckled.

"Jonah!" shouted Alex. "God told him to go to, uh, some city. . . ."

"Nineveh," Mother helped her.

"Oh, yeah, Nineveh," Alex continued, "and Jonah didn't want to go so he got on a ship to go somewhere else. Then God sent a huge storm and the men on the ship threw Jonah overboard and a big fish swallowed him!"

"Do you remember how long Jonah stayed inside that fish, Firecracker?" asked Father.

"Three days and three nights," Alex answered.

"Jonah certainly had a rough time when he disobeyed God, didn't he?" added Father. "How about you, Steamroller? Can you think of anyone who did not obey God?''

Rudy rolled his eyes. He was thinking hard. Barbara leaned over to him and whispered something in his ear.

"Oh, yeah," he cried. "That lady! That lady that turned to salt."

Father and Mother smiled at each other. Alex and Barbara giggled. "Do you mean Lot's wife?" Father asked Rudy.

"Yeah, Lot's wife. She looked back at the city that was burning. The angels had told her not to, but she did anyway, and she was turned into a big high, oh, you know . . ." Rudy couldn't think of the word. He looked to Father for help.

"A pillar," Father prompted him.

"Yeah, a pillar. She turned into a pillar of salt." Rudy pointed at his mother. "Mom, if we ever have to leave our house 'cuz it's on fire, don't look back! Just don't look back!"

Everybody howled with laughter. Rudy looked confused. He was serious. He did not want his mother turned into a pillar of salt.

"Don't worry, Rudy," soothed Mother, as she put her arms around him. "If any angels tell me not to look back, I won't look back. I promise."

Father smiled and said, "We have seen good things that happen when people obey God and bad things that happen when people don't obey God. God wants us to obey Him, but like everything else, we have to learn how to obey. Sometimes that can be hard work. So God gave us certain people on earth that we must obey to help us learn obedience. Who do you think those people are?"

"We have to obey the police," suggested Barbara.

"That's right. Anybody else?" Father asked.

"Teachers," called Alex.

"Yeah, teachers!" agreed Rudy. He folded his arms across his chest and wrinkled his nose.

"Teachers and police are good answers," agreed Father, "but I'm thinking of two special people that God gives to children to teach them how to obey."

"Oh," said Barbara, nodding her head, "you mean our parents!"

"Ohhhhhh," echoed Alex and Rudy. Rudy remembered Barbara's world map he had almost ruined and Alex remembered the five dollars she shouldn't have spent at the carnival.

"Well, goodness, you two," their mother laughed. "You look like you expect us to tell you to jump off a bridge or something!"

Father chuckled. "Obeying your parents isn't so bad. God says in the Bible, 'Children, obey your parents in the Lord, for this is right.' So you see, by obeying your parents, you are also obeying God. And what happens when we obey God?"

"Good things!" they all shouted together.

CHAPTER 6

The Valley of the Shadow of Death

Alex awoke the next morning with the sun streaming through her bedroom window. She stretched, then suddenly rose straight up in bed. Her alarm! It hadn't awakened her at midnight!

Alex checked the clock on her radio. Yes, the alarm was set at 12. Why didn't it go off?

Her mother appeared in the doorway. "Oh, you're awake," she said. "Did your alarm go off?"

"No, I just woke up on my own," yawned Alex.

"Well, I know why it hasn't gone off these last two mornings," declared Mother. "Somehow it was set wrong. The goofy thing went off at midnight last night. I had to come in here and turn it off. I'm surprised you slept through all that racket.''

After Mother left the room, Alex sat on the edge of her bed and stared at the floor. Part of her wanted to tell her mother what had really happened to the alarm and part of her didn't. She knew that if her mother asked if she'd set the alarm at midnight, she would have to tell her the truth. There had been a time, not long ago, that Alex had found herself in trouble because of several lies she had told. Since that time, she had promised herself and the Lord that she would never tell a lie again.

''Brussels sprouts,'' Alex told herself. ''Mom doesn't even suspect that I set the alarm for midnight. She trusts me not to do things like that. I wonder what she'd think if she knew that I sneaked downstairs in the middle of the night or that I hid in the janitor's closet or that I spent that five dollars at the carnival? If she knew all that, she'd probably never trust me again!''

Alex began pulling on her clothes. She could hear her father singing in the shower. ''At least he sounds happy.'' she grumbled. ''Guess it's no lunch and the janitor's closet for me today. It's awful sitting in the dark by myself! Well, I'll just say the 23rd Psalm again. I wonder if I should ask Dad about the valley of the shadow of death?"

Just then the bathroom door opened.

"Dad?" Alex called.

Her father, dressed in his bathrobe, stuck his head in her doorway. "Good morning, Firecracker."

"Dad, I've been wondering about the 23rd Psalm," began Alex.

"At six thirty in the morning?" her father exclaimed.

"Yeah," Alex replied with a shrug of her shoulders. "You see there's a part of it that I don't like to say."

Father walked over to Alex's bed and sat down beside her. "What part is that, Firecracker?"

"The scary part," Alex answered quickly.

"The scary part?" asked Father, puzzled.

"Yeah, you know," Alex exclaimed, "the valley of the shadow of death!"

"Oh," Father's eyes twinkled. "I remember a time when that was the scary part for me, too."

He put his arm around Alex and hugged her close to him.

"You know, Firecracker, sometimes we feel afraid. Maybe we are even in danger. Or perhaps we are very worried about something. I call those troubled times the 'valleys.' "

"You mean like the valley of the shadow of death?" Alex interrupted.

"Exactly," Father replied. "We all have valleys in our lives. But no matter how dark those valleys may seem, we can go through them without fear by trusting Jesus to guide us.

"The Bible tells us that Jesus is our Shepherd and we are His sheep. What does a shepherd do for his sheep?"

"Well, he walks with them," replied Alex.

"Right," agreed Father, "and what else does he do for his sheep?"

"He watches them," Alex answered again.

"He walks with them and watches them to keep them from harm," Father nodded. "A shepherd scares off enemies that try to attack his sheep, and he makes sure that his sheep stay on the right path. That's what Jesus does for us, too. He scares off our enemies and keeps us on the right path through the valleys in our lives."

"Why do we have to go through those creepy valleys anyway?" wondered Alex.

"To get to the top of the mountain, of course," Father grinned at Alex.

"Huh? What do you mean? What mountain?" asked Alex.

"Every spring," Father told her, "a shepherd leads his sheep to higher ground. He wants to get them to the mountaintop to their summer fields of grass. The easiest way to climb a mountain is to go through the valleys along the mountain's slope.''

"But what does that have to do with us?" Alex was puzzled. "We aren't climbing any mountain!"

"Oh, but indeed we are, Firecracker," Father told her. "We are climbing the mountain of faith. Every time we allow Jesus, our Shepherd, to lead us through the valleys, we increase our trust in Him. Just like a flock of sheep has to depend on its shepherd to get them through the valleys, so we have to depend on our Shepherd. That builds faith and we climb higher up the faith mountain.''

"Brussels sprouts," Alex cried. "That almost makes me want to go through more valleys!"

Father laughed. "This may sound strange, Firecracker, but the more valleys we go through, the stronger we get and the higher up the mountain we climb.''

A sudden loud voice broke into their conversation. "WHAT ARE YOU TWO DOING?" Mother stood in the doorway, hands on her hips, staring in amazement at Father and Alex.

"Do you know what time it is?" Mother went on. "You're both going to be late! Neither one of you is dressed and I already have breakfast on the table." Mother tapped her foot in pretend anger.

"We were having a very important conversation," Father explained to Mother. He winked at Alex and hurried out of the room.

Alex rushed around her room, hurriedly grabbing her shoes and socks. She was so glad that she had talked with her father. She felt much better about having to sit in the janitor's closet today. She would go through that valley with her Shepherd!

The rest of the morning went quickly—too quickly—and soon Alex found herself lining up with her class for lunch. Lorraine gave Alex a sympathetic look as she stepped behind Lorraine at the end of the line. Lorraine was always the last one in line. She was too shy to move ahead of anyone else.

Alex felt her knees shake as she followed the line down the hallway. Could she escape her teacher's keen eyes again and duck into the janitor's closet without being noticed?

As the line moved past the closet door, Alex glanced at Mrs. Tuttle. Her teacher was not looking. Alex quietly sidestepped to the door and whisked inside.

Darkness covered her. "I will not be afraid," she told herself. "Yea, though I walk through the valley of the shadow of death, I will fear no evil: for thou art with me; thy rod and thy staff they comfort me!"

As Alex repeated the words over and over, she began to imagine a shaded mountain valley with green grass and a beautiful mountain stream running through it. The picture of the valley brought Alex a feeling of calmness and peace. In fact, she felt so peaceful that she decided to step farther into the darkness and explore the closet.

Alex took a few careful steps deeper into the closet and slowly stretched her arms out on both sides. She felt nothing. Keeping her arms extended, Alex stepped farther and farther into the closet. Suddenly, her left arm brushed against something. It felt like a pole. Probably nothing but an old broom, Alex decided. She tried to grab it. It slipped sideways and knocked into something beside it. That "something" slipped sideways and hit something else. Before Alex knew it, everything on the left side of the closet was falling noisily to the floor! Something crashed into Alex. She lost her balance and tumbled over.

CHAPTER 7

Crash!
Crack!
Smash!
Shatter!

Alex hit the floor hard. Thuds, clangs, and bangs sounded everywhere. It seemed like the entire closet was collapsing around her! Something soft and squishy and rather damp flopped across her face.

"YEEACK!" Alex pulled what felt like a mop off of her face and slung it sideways. BANG! It hit the wall.

Alex didn't make another move. She lay on the floor of the closet listening for footsteps. Surely everyone in the school building had heard the uproar.

Twenty-five . . . fifty . . . one hundred seconds and no footsteps. Alex counted another one hundred seconds. All was quiet. She began to relax.

"Tap! Tap! Tap!"

What was that?

"Tap! Tap! Tap!"

It sounded like someone tapping on the door! Alex froze.

"Alex? A-l-e-x?" called a soft voice. Was that Janie?

"Alex! Hurry up and open the door!" The voice demanded. It was Janie's voice.

Alex sprang off the floor and started for the door. BANG! CRASH! "OUCH!" She tripped over something. Alex rubbed her knee. Hobbling to the door, she felt for the doorknob and opened the door cautiously, just a crack.

"Janie?"

"Alex? What took you so long? Here, I brought you something. Hold out your hands."

With her eyes wide open in amazement, Alex shoved her arms out the door. Janie dropped something warm into her hands, turned, and fled down the hall.

Alex looked down. A hot dog! Janie had brought her a hot dog. Brussels sprouts!

Alex grinned and quickly backed into the closet, closing the door behind her. She ate the hot

dog in three big bites.

"RRRIIINNNGGG!" The loud blast of the school bell made Alex jump and cover her ears.

Once again, Alex waited for her teacher and her class to pass by the crack in the closet door. Once again, she crept with shaky legs behind Lorraine at the end of the line. Once again, she passed by a suspicious-looking Mrs. Tuttle at the door to the playground.

"Alex?" her teacher held out a hand. "I don't remember seeing you in the lunchroom."

Alex skidded to a stop. Her mouth opened

wide. She stared at her teacher, not knowing what to say. Quite by accident, she must have looked innocent to Mrs. Tuttle. Her teacher shrugged her shoulders and said, "I must have just missed seeing you. Go on out to recess."

Alex stumbled out the door to her waiting friends. "I better not hide in that closet anymore," she told them. "Mrs. Tuttle almost caught me!"

Late that afternoon, Alex trudged up the hill to her house. She had just come from softball practice. Usually softball practice filled her with energy, but today she was tired. Alex decided that was because she was so hungry.

When Alex reached home, she collapsed on her back on the top step of the front porch. Backpack, books, and softball mitt tumbled down the steps where she dropped them.

"Alex's home! Come on!" Two pair of eager feet clattered up the driveway, up the walk, up the steps, and with a plop, landed on either side of Alex's head. Alex did not have to open her eyes to know who belonged to those feet.

"Goblin," she groaned, "I am too tired."

"Aw, Alex, come on," pleaded Rudy.

"Please, Alex," begged another voice.

Alex squinted at Rudy and his best friend, Jason. Jason lived next door to Alex and Rudy. Alex liked Jason. He was easier to get along with than her brother. Alex often wondered if that was because his father was a minister. Maybe spending so much time at church made Jason a neat kid.

Both boys bent over Alex and peered at her face. They wore such pitiful looks on their faces that Alex chuckled.

"Oh, she's just teasing us, Jason," Rudy said in relief.

"No, I'm not, Goblin," insisted Alex. "I'm too hot and tired and hungry and thirsty to practice softball with you."

Rudy frowned at Jason. He and Jason needed Alex's help. They were going to start playing Little League ball next week for the first time.

Suddenly, Rudy's face brightened. "Wait right here, Alex," he ordered. "Don't go away!"

Rudy banged open the front door and disappeared into the house. In a few moments he returned hugging a banana, a chocolate cupcake, and a tall glass of ice water in his arms.

"There!" Rudy proudly plopped the goodies down beside Alex. "That'll make you feel better."

Alex stared at her brother in surprise. There were times when she actually liked the little brat. This was one of those times.

"Thanks, Goblin," Alex muttered, grabbing the ice water and gulping down half of it. She quickly wolfed down the banana. She ate the cupcake slowly to make it last as long as possible. After drinking the rest of the ice water, Alex had to admit she did feel better.

The boys sat on the step beside her, anxiously watching her every move. Finally, Rudy could stand it no longer. "Well," he cried. "Do you feel like playing now?"

Alex turned her head very slowly and looked at her brother. She teased him by not answering right away. Suddenly, she grabbed her softball mitt off the bottom step and ran out into the middle of the yard.

"BATTER UP!" she hollered.

Rudy and Jason shouted with glee and ran with Alex to the backyard. Their own small softball diamond sat in the farthest corner of the yard, its base paths worn smooth by active feet. The V of the fence corner served as the backstop. The pitcher's mound had been raised by many wagon loads of dirt.

Alex stood on her own pitcher's mound. This was a favorite place. She loved to pitch. She was the star pitcher for her own team, the Tornadoes.

Jason batted first.

"Choke up on the bat more, Jason!" Alex called.

Jason quickly moved his hands up on the bat. He always followed Alex's advice. Alex was the best ballplayer he knew.

Alex threw some pitches. Jason missed more than he hit.

"Put your hands together, Jason!

"Watch the ball, Jason!"

"My turn!" Rudy announced loudly. He was tired of fielding.

"Just a minute! Just a minute!" Alex hollered. She quickly strode to the plate and grabbed the bat out of Jason's hands.

"Now, watch," she told Rudy and Jason. "See, I put my feet here like this—not too close and not too far from the plate. Then, I bring my left foot close to my right foot so when the ball comes in, I can step sideways into the pitch. That gives me more power."

Jason and Rudy watched intently as Alex demonstrated her batting position. Alex was extremely serious when it came to softball. It was a very important activity in her life.

"When you hold a bat, keep your hands together." Alex held the bat over her shoulder. "Choke up on the bat if it feels too long or heavy. The higher you choke up on it, the faster you can swing!" Alex swung the bat a few times.

"When you swing a bat," Alex continued, "swing it level and swing it smooth. Don't try to kill the ball, just try to meet the ball with the bat. Never take your eyes off the ball!" She stared at the boys to see if they understood. They nodded their heads.

"Let me try!" cried Rudy.

Alex handed him the bat with an I-hope-you-paid-attention look on her face.

Rudy took some time getting ready to swing. He was trying to imitate Alex's every example. He took a few practice swings.

"Ready?" Alex called from the mound. Rudy nodded. His face was set with a determined look. Alex went into her windup. She held the ball in her right hand, drew both hands up to her chest, blew a bubble with her gum, leaned to the right, threw her right arm in two circles behind her and her left leg in front of her, popped the bubble, bent her left knee, leaned forward, and released the ball.

It flew straight over home plate.

"CRACK!" went Rudy's bat.

The ball soared up, up, higher and higher, over Alex's head, over Jason's head, and over the fence! The children watched it excitedly. Rudy hopped about in joy. He had hit the ball well!

All in an instant, the happy looks on the children's faces turned to looks of horror. The ball was heading straight into the glass porch at the back of Jason's house!

Jason covered his eyes. Rudy covered his ears.

Alex pointed at the ball, opened her mouth, but no sound came out.

"CRASH! CRACK! SMASH! SHATTER!" The noise was terrible. Pieces of glass flew as one enormous pane crunched to the ground!

For a moment, none of them could move. Then, panic gripped the children. Alex, Rudy, and Jason raced out of the backyard and into the front yard, dropping behind some bushes to hide.

CHAPTER 8

Listen to My Heart?

Alex, Rudy, and Jason crouched low behind a row of bushes in Alex's front yard. Peeking through the branches, they saw Jason's mother run to her backyard. They heard her cries of alarm as she discovered the now-ruined glass porch. The children held their breath as they heard Alex's mother join Jason's mother in the backyard. A few minutes later both mothers began calling their children's names.

"Come on, Rudy! Mom's calling us! We have to go!" Alex began crawling out of the bushes, dragging Rudy behind her.

"Do we have to, Alex?" Rudy clung to a branch, making it impossible for Alex to pull him any further.

Alex looked at her brother. "What else are we going to do? Spend the night here in the bushes?

We shouldn't have run away in the first place. We should have stayed there and explained what happened.''

"ALEX! RUDY!" Their mother sounded angry.

"JASON!" shouted his mother.

"Alex is right, Rudy. We better go!" Jason scrambled out of the bushes.

"You're not the one who smashed in your porch, Jason," Rudy replied hotly. "I'm the one who'll get in all the trouble!"

"Look, it wasn't your fault," Alex told Rudy.

"I mean, it wasn't like you broke the porch on purpose. We'll go with you, and I'll do the talking, okay?"

"Oh, okay," grumbled Rudy. He slowly followed Alex out of the bushes.

Just then a car pulled into the driveway. It was Father coming home from work.

"Oh, no!" Rudy exclaimed. Alex held onto his hand tightly to keep him from diving back under the bushes.

As Father was getting out of his car, another car pulled into Jason's driveway. It was Jason's father.

Alex felt Jason quickly grab her other hand. Rudy's lips began to quiver as tears streamed down his face. Alex felt frightened, too. Trying to explain a broken porch to two angry mothers was hard enough, but explaining it to two angry mothers and two angry fathers was worse!

At that instant, the mothers strode around the corner of the house and found their children. "ALEX! RUDY! JASON!"

"What's going on?" Father asked as he gazed at three frightened children and two upset mothers. Jason's father joined the group.

"Follow us!" both mothers commanded. They led the way to Jason's backyard. Father, Jason's father, Jason, Alex, and Rudy walked behind them.

"Oh, no!" Father cried, as he saw the damaged porch.

"What happened?" exclaimed Jason's father.

"That's what I'd like to know. We found a softball in the middle of the broken glass!" Mother folded her arms across her chest and stared at the three children.

No one said anything for a long minute. Alex knew it was up to her to start talking, but there was a big lump in her throat. She cleared her throat several times.

"Well, see, uh," she choked. "I was helping Rudy and Jason with their batting and, well, Rudy hit the ball real good and it sorta flew into the porch. He didn't mean to do it!"

When she finished speaking, Alex was surprised to see a grin spreading across her father's face. He couldn't keep back his chuckles. Mother glared at him.

"I'm sorry, I can't help it!" laughed Father. "I remember doing the same thing when I was a boy, only I didn't break a glass porch. I slugged one through the school window. Hit old man Wilcox as he stood in front of the blackboard teaching sixth-grade math. Boy, did he ever get mad!"

"HA, HA, HA, HA!" roared Jason's father. "I did better'n that! The first ball I hit through a window flew into a grocery store. Landed in a big barrel full of pickles. Pickle juice ran through those aisles!"

The two men laughed hilariously at each other. The mothers looked at each other and shook their heads. The children began to smile. Things didn't seem as bad now.

When the laughter died down, Mother said to the children, "I understand how it happened, but after you broke the glass, you should not have run away. Even though you did not mean to break the glass, you still broke it. When something bad happens because of something you do, you need to admit it and try to do whatever you can to make it right again."

"I'm sorry," Alex apologized. "I know it was wrong for us to run and hide in the bushes. Even when I was running away, I knew it was wrong. I couldn't stop myself. I was too scared."

"I understand," replied Mother, smiling down at her.

"So do I," Jason's father added. He squatted down in front of the three children. "Alex said something that interests me," he told them. "She said that she knew she should not have run away, but she did so anyway because she was afraid. What about you, Jason and Rudy? Did you think it was right to run after you broke the glass?"

"No," Jason and Rudy answered together.

"Let me ask you another question," said Jason's father. "You usually know when you are doing something good, don't you?"

"Yes," the children agreed.

"And, you usually know when you are doing something bad, don't you?"

The children nodded their heads.

Jason's father smiled at the children. "That is your heart speaking to you," he told them.

They looked at him with astonished faces. He

laughed. "You see, God wants us to do good, so He gave each one of us the ability to know what is right and what is wrong. He planted that knowledge deep down in our hearts.

"You need to listen to your heart and do what it tells you is the right thing to do even when you're afraid. Don't let the fear rob you of the joy that you get from doing the right thing."

As Jason's father talked, Alex felt a kind of "jump" inside of her. Was that her heart telling her to listen to it? Something had been telling her that hiding in the janitor's closet was wrong. So was sneaking downstairs at midnight to make her lunch. Other bad things had happened too—like her sister being blamed for the peanut butter mess in the kitchen. And even Alex's being too tired and hungry to play well at softball practice. It all came from spending that five dollars at the carnival. She wished she had obeyed her mother and her heart!

"Well," her father's voice broke into her thoughts. "I think you owe Jason's parents an apology." He looked sternly at Alex and Rudy.

"I'm sorry," Alex and Rudy responded.

"Me, too," added Jason.

"Has anyone thought of who is going to pay to get the porch fixed?" Father raised his eyebrows at the children.

"Uh," Alex dug in the dirt with her toe. "I only have a dollar and thirty-seven cents in my bank. I'm sure that's not enough."

"Well, I have two quarters and three nickels and seven pennies," Rudy added proudly.

"How much does that make, Rudy?" chuckled Father.

"Oh, about a dollar," guessed Rudy. The grownups laughed.

"I only have three cents," voiced Jason. "I spent all my money on food for Clementine and Homer." Clementine and Homer were Jason's pet turtles.

"How much does glass cost anyway, Dad?" Jason asked his father. "Do we have enough?"

"Hmm," Jason's father stroked his chin. "With the insurance money, you might have enough." More chuckles came from the grownups.

Insurance! There is that word again, thought

Alex. She remembered her parents had talked about insurance when she had accidently whomped her father's car with a wagon load of rocks. "Insurance must be something parents get when their kids mess up and wreck something," Alex told herself. "Maybe it's a kind of reward for having to put up with clumsy kids."

Alex and Rudy followed their parents inside. It was dinnertime. Alex made sure to help her mother in the kitchen. It was always good to help out parents after you had made them mad. Even Rudy set the table with no complaints.

That night in bed, Alex decided that she was going to listen to her heart, and she was going to do what her heart told her to do. After all, God was the Maker of her heart. If she listened to it, she would really be listening to Him.

She did not set her alarm for midnight. It was wrong to sneak downstairs at midnight. What about hiding in the janitor's closet? Her heart told her that was also wrong. What else could she do? Tell her parents everything? Not tonight! Not after breaking a glass porch.

Alex flopped over to her stomach and wiggled

into her favorite sleeping position. She was too tired to think about it tonight. She would think about it tomorrow. She hugged her stuffed Garfield tightly and fell fast asleep.

CHAPTER 9

Caught at Last

The next morning, Alex did not have much time to worry about lunch. Mrs. Tuttle kept the class busy with reading and math and spelling. She hurried the class through their lessons. A speaker was going to visit them later that morning. The speaker's name was Mrs. Popham, and she was going to talk about Kansas history.

Alex was tired of hearing about her state's history. If one more person told her about sod houses and covered wagons and the Santa Fe Trail, Alex thought she just might scream. She hoped Mrs. Popham would not bring them a sunflower to color. If one more person gave her a sunflower to color, Alex was going to color it purple.

When Mrs. Popham entered the classroom, she carried a chart under her left arm. On the chart, Alex could see a curvy dotted line marked "Santa Fe Trail." Alex quickly covered her mouth to stop any screams that might come out of it. Mrs. Popham also balanced a small sod house and covered wagon in her hands.

Mrs. Popham was a tiny, silver-haired lady who looked like she might really have lived in the pioneer days. She said she was going to tell the class about how her great-great-grandmother traveled in a covered wagon many hundreds of miles, and how her great-great-grandmother helped to build a sod house, and how her great-great-grandmother lived in that sod house for years and years.

The class listened to Mrs. Popham tell of hardships and troubles experienced while journeying west. About the time in Mrs. Popham's story when the poor, tired oxen pulled the covered wagon out of the third muddy river, Alex felt a tap on her shoulder.

"Hey, Alex! Look!" whispered Chrissy, who sat behind her.

Alex turned around and almost shouted out loud. Eddie Thompson had his hand in one of the hermit crab terrariums and was slowly pulling out a crab! He set it on the floor and tapped his foot behind it. The hermit crab began a frightened crawl toward the front of the classroom.

That dumb Eddie Thompson! Of course, he had picked Alex's terrarium and that was her crab, Sandpan, crawling on the floor. Eddie Thompson had always been jealous of Sandpan because he was the biggest and fastest hermit crab in the class.

Sandpan! Poor Sandpan! The crab would stop and try to hide in his shell, but there was always some boy nearby to tap a foot behind him and make him crawl on.

All the children watched Sandpan out of the corners of their eyes. A few giggles sounded now and then, but Mrs. Popham thought the class was laughing at the funny parts of her story and she would laugh with them. Mrs. Tuttle kept glancing at the children with puzzled looks, but because Sandpan was too little for her to notice on the classroom floor, the teacher did not discover the true reason for their laughter.

Alex almost wished Mrs. Tuttle would see Sandpan. She'd rather have her teacher angry than have something horrible happen to her hermit crab. What if he got squished or something? Alex had taken good care of Sandpan. He was getting used to her touch and didn't even hide in his shell anymore when she picked him up. Now these stupid boys were making him afraid again and ruining everything!

Should she get up and rescue Sandpan? He was almost to the front of the room. Too late. Allen Jacobs, who sat in the front row, snatched up the crab.

Slyly grinning at the other boys, he waited until Mrs. Tuttle was not looking and Mrs. Popham was pointing at her chart. He then quickly placed Sandpan on top of the table where the sod house and covered wagon sat.

Mrs. Popham left her chart and walked over to the table. She was ready to demonstrate how to build a sod house. Sandpan sat a few inches away from the house. He was drawn into his shell. He looked like a plain ordinary seashell.

"Oh, my goodness!" Mrs. Popham exclaimed. "Whatever is a seashell doing here?"

At that moment, several things happened at once: Mrs. Popham picked up the shell. Sandpan peeked out of the shell. Alex jumped out of her chair. Mrs. Popham screamed! Alex ran forward. Mrs. Popham flung the shell away from her! Alex dove over two desks and caught Sandpan in midair!

"Alexandria Brackenbury!" exclaimed Mrs. Tuttle.

Alex lay on the floor and clutched Sandpan,

hoping desperately that the crab was all right. "It wasn't my fault," she managed to tell Mrs. Tuttle.

"That's right!" one of the girls shouted. "Eddie Thompson took her crab out of the terrarium!"

"Yeah, and Allen Jacobs put it up on the table!" cried another girl.

Instantly, all the girls in the class began talking at once, loudly explaining to Mrs. Tuttle what had happened.

Mrs. Tuttle held up her hands. Everyone quieted down.

"Eddie Thompson and Allen Jacobs will come with me!" she ordered. "Alex, please put your crab back in its terrarium."

"Oh, let me see if he's okay" wailed Alex. She was almost in tears. Sandpan had completely disappeared into his shell and wouldn't move even when she touched him.

"All right," Mrs. Tuttle sighed, "take him to your desk. I'm sorry, Mrs. Popham, please go on with your talk." The teacher left the room with Eddie Thompson and Allen Jacobs.

Mrs. Popham nervously continued speaking. Alex did not hear one word. She was overjoyed when Sandpan finally decided to take a crawl on her hand.

Mrs. Tuttle soon returned without the two boys. Mrs. Popham finished speaking and passed out a sheet of paper to each child. Alex looked at hers. It was an outline of a giant sunflower!

Alex was looking for her purple crayon when Mrs. Tuttle announced that it was lunchtime. Alex quickly put Sandpan back into his terrarium. She'd forgotten all about lunch in the excitement of the morning. What was she going to do? She knew she wasn't supposed to hide in the janitor's closet anymore. But the only other thing she could do was to tell her teacher that she didn't have any lunch. Her teacher would ask her why she didn't have any lunch. She would have to explain everything to Mrs. Tuttle. It would be easier to hide in the janitor's closet one more time. Alex ran to the back of the line behind Lorraine.

When the class marched passed the janitor's closet, Alex tiptoed sideways and reached for the closet's doorknob. It wouldn't turn. The door was locked! Alex twisted and turned the knob frantically.

A hand suddenly clamped down on Alex's shoulder! "So this is the closet burglar," growled a low voice. Alex twisted around to see Mr. Whitney, the school's janitor, standing over her.

"I'm not a burglar," she squeaked.

"You don't say?" retorted Mr. Whitney. "Well, someone got into my closet yesterday and just about tore it to pieces! Wouldn't have been you, would it?" Mr. Whitney glared at her.

"I didn't mean to tear up your closet. I was only hiding." Alex was terribly afraid. It was all over now. She had been caught!

"Hiding? What were you hiding from?" asked Mr. Whitney.

Alex couldn't answer. She knew if she tried to say one more word, tears would flood her face.

"Well, hmmmpf," Mr. Whitney snorted, "you better talk this over with Mrs. Larson. Come along now."

Mrs. Larson was the school principal. Mr.

Whitney and Alex walked down the hall to her office. They had to pass by the cafeteria. Alex stared straight ahead. She didn't dare look in the cafeteria window. She hoped Mrs. Tuttle wouldn't see her.

"We need to see the principal," Mr. Whitney announced to the office secretary. The secretary gave Mr. Whitney and Alex a surprised look. Alex wished there were a hole she could fall into and disappear.

"I believe Mrs. Larson will be right out," the secretary told them.

A moment later, the principal's door opened. Out stepped Mrs. Larson, Eddie Thompson, and Allen Jacobs. Alex ducked her head and scrunched as close to the wall as she could. She hoped the boys wouldn't notice her.

"Okay, boys, you may go eat lunch now, but report to your teacher at recess time," ordered Mrs. Larson. "She'll make sure you have something to do besides causing mischief."

Both boys turned toward the door. They had to pass by Alex on their way out.

"ALEX!" they cried when they saw her.

Alex didn't answer or look at them. She couldn't. She couldn't look at anyone. Her face reddened and she tried hard to blink back the tears that were already blurring all the colors of the carpet together. She felt like a criminal. For what seemed like forever, Mrs. Larson, Mr. Whitney, the office secretary, Eddie Thompson, and Allen Jacobs stood and stared at her.

CHAPTER 10

Higher Up the Mountain

"WHAT ARE YOU DOING HERE?" hollered Eddie Thompson and Allen Jacobs. They each pointed a finger at Alex.

Alex leaned against the wall of the school office. She was so ashamed. She could hardly stand up.

"That is none of your business," Mrs. Larson told the boys. She sent them out of the office.

"Well, Mr. Whitney, what may I do for you and Alex?" the principal asked.

"Caught this little girl trying to get into my closet," Mr. Whitney reported.

"What?" exclaimed Mrs. Larson.

"Caught her trying to get into my closet," Mr. Whitney repeated. "She's the one that wrecked up the place yesterday."

"Not Alex!" Mrs. Larson cried.

"Afraid so," mumbled the janitor, rubbing his chin. "Said she was hiding."

"Hiding?" Mrs. Larson looked confused. "Well, Alex, I think we'd better talk about this. Come on inside my office. Thank you, Mr. Whitney."

Mr. Whitney left the office, still rubbing his chin. Alex forced her rubbery legs to follow the principal into her office.

"Alex, I can hardly believe this about you," said Mrs. Larson.

"Me, neither," mumbled Alex, finally finding her voice. "It's sorta unbelievable."

"Oh, dear. Well, suppose you tell me why you were hiding in the janitor's closet." Mrs. Larson smiled such a friendly smile that Alex lost some of her fear.

Alex poured out her story to the principal. She told her about the carnival and the five dollars that she shouldn't have spent and hiding in the janitor's closet and making her lunch at midnight.

"Goodness, Alex," Mrs. Larson said when Alex had finished. "It sounds like you've been through a few rough days." She patted Alex's hand. "I can tell you feel bad about the whole thing."

Alex nodded her head. "I'm sorry about messing up the janitor's closet," she gulped.

Mrs. Larson chuckled, "I think we will have you help Mr. Whitney during one of your recesses tomorrow. There should be some little job that you could help him with. That should make him feel better about having his closet 'wrecked up,' as he puts it."

Alex nodded again. Help Mr. Whitney? How could she help Mr. Whitney? She wasn't very good at mopping floors.

"I will explain all of this to your teacher, Alex," promised Mrs. Larson. "But you will have to explain it to your parents. I'll call them later and say that you have something to tell them. That way, when you get home, you can tell them about it in your own words."

Alex sighed. Telling her parents was going to be hard.

"Here's a pass so that you can go eat lunch, Alex. You'll have to eat with the fifth and sixth graders. I'm sure your regular lunch period is over by now. After you eat, you can return to your class." Mrs. Larson smiled at her. "Thank you for telling me what happened, Alex. I think everything will turn out all right."

When Alex got back to her classroom, she reached the door just as the other children were coming in from recess.

"Alex! Where were you?" Janie asked.

Alex quickly shushed her. She did not want everyone in the class to know about her visit to the principal. Eddie Thompson and Allen Jacobs grinned wickedly at her. She ignored them. They had nothing to grin at her about. After all, they had just spent their recess with Mrs. Tuttle.

The afternoon pressed on. Alex spent most of it worrying. Had Mrs. Larson called her parents? What did she say to them?

The last bell of the day rang. Alex pulled Janie out the door. She waited until Rudy and Jason were far ahead of them before she told Janie all that had happened. The two girls wondered what Alex's parents would say and do. Alex hoped she wouldn't be grounded for too long.

As soon as her father came home from work, Mother sent Rudy next door to play with Jason. Barbara was at a friend's house. Alex was alone with her parents.

Alex sat nervously on the edge of a chair in the living room. Her father sat down across from her in another chair. Her mother seated herself on the sofa.

"Well, Firecracker," her father broke the silence. "Your principal called today."

"Yes, Mrs. Larson said you had something to tell us," added Mother.

"Oh, uh, yeah," stuttered Alex. She shifted in her chair. She wondered what had happened to her voice. It sounded dry and raspy and kind of far away—not like her own voice at all.

"Just start at the beginning," her mother encouraged her. "Once you get started, it'll be easier."

Alex swallowed hard. "Okay, uh, remember that ten dollars you gave me to take to the carnival?"

Her mother looked surprised but nodded her head.

"And, uh, remember how I was only s'posed to spend five dollars of it?"

Her mother nodded again.

"Well, see, Janie and I were real upset by the haunted house and we used up all our money except the last five dollars and Janie wanted to do the Cake Walk again and I felt bad because she couldn't do it. Well, anyway, I spent all the money!" Alex ducked her head and waited for her parents to yell.

No one yelled. No one even spoke for a long minute. Then Mother said, "That means you didn't have any lunch money this week. What did you do for lunches?"

"Uh, hmmph," Alex cleared her throat. "I hid in the janitor's closet at lunch."

"What?" exclaimed Mother.

"You hid in the janitor's closet every day this week?" asked Father in amazement.

"Well, not exactly," Alex told him. "Today I didn't 'cuz I got caught by the janitor, and one day I took my lunch."

"You took your lunch?" questioned Mother. "I don't remember making a lunch for you to take to school this week."

"You didn't make it, Mom. I made it. I, uh, sorta made it at midnight." Alex ducked her head again.

"Midnight!" both parents cried.

"Yeah, I set my alarm for midnight and came downstairs and made my lunch."

"That's why your alarm went off at midnight," Mother said. She looked at Father and they both sighed.

"And Barbara got blamed for the peanut butter mess the next morning and it was really me that made it," Alex added.

"Oh, dear," Mother sighed again. "But, Alex," she asked, "weren't you afraid to go downstairs at midnight?"

"Yes," Alex admitted. "I was afraid to turn off the lamp in the living room. I kept wishing I had a light I could carry around with me everywhere."

"You do, Firecracker," Father said. "Jesus is your Light, and He goes with you everywhere."

Alex thought about that for a moment. "Yeah," she said slowly. "I know He was in the janitor's closet with me. He helped me feel better, especially when I said the 23rd Psalm.''

"The 23rd Psalm!" exclaimed Father. "So that's why you asked me about it."

"Oh, yeah," Alex replied. "It was really dark in the closet and I was sorta scared and the only thing I could think of to say was the 23rd Psalm. But I didn't like that part about the valley of the shadow of death 'cuz I didn't understand about the valleys.''

"Do you understand now?" Father asked.

"I think so." Alex was silent for a few moments. Then she added, "I think I've been going through a really big valley, but now I'm at the end of it."

"Why do you say that, Firecracker?" asked Father.

"Well, because I've learned so much. It sounds funny, but I even feel older."

"What have you learned, Alex?" her mother asked.

"Well, now I know how important it is to obey your parents and that when you obey your parents, you're also obeying God. I mean, none of

this would've happened if I'd saved the five dollars like you told me to.''

''Hmmmpf!'' Father looked surprised. ''I talked about obeying God and obeying parents the other night because Rudy had disobeyed us and used Barbara's poster paint. I didn't know that you had so much need for that lesson, Firecracker.''

''The Lord knew she needed to hear it,'' said Mother. ''It sounds like He's been guiding you through this whole thing,'' she told Alex.

''Yeah, and I guess I knew all along that He

wanted me to stop hiding and sneaking around and tell you all about it, but I didn't listen to Him 'cuz I was too scared. Just like yesterday when we broke the glass porch. I was too scared and I ran away." Alex hung her head. "I guess I'm not a very good sheep."

Her parents laughed.

"Not true, Firecracker, not true," boomed Father. "You are just as good a sheep as any of us. We all make mistakes. That's why we need our Shepherd to lead us . . . and to get us out of sticky situations."

"Yeah, He got me out of this one all right," exclaimed Alex. "I just hope that next time something happens, I'll listen to my heart and to my Shepherd."

"You'll get better and better at it," laughed her mother. "You see, Jesus not only leads us through the valleys, but He teaches us as we go. That's what it means to grow up in the Lord. Remember, you said a little while ago that you felt older? You are older. Every time you learn something from the Lord, your faith grows."

"And I climb higher up the mountain!" shouted Alex. Her face shone with excitement. "Brussels sprouts! All this time I've been climbing the faith mountain and I didn't even know it!"

Alex felt sudden tears in her eyes. She looked at her parents and saw tears in their eyes, too. At the same time, she and her father moved to sit by Mother on the sofa. All three hugged each other tightly.

"God is so good," whispered Mother.

Amen.

T-Bone Trouble

Nancy Simpson Levene

Chariot Books™

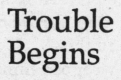

CHAPTER 1

Trouble Begins

Alex stood silently in the middle of her bedroom floor. Had she heard someone call for help? Motioning for her friend Melissa to be quiet, Alex listened again. There was no doubt about it. A faint "Help! Help!" met her ears. It sounded as if it was coming from the direction of the upstairs bathroom.

Alex snapped her fingers. "Of course!" she said.

"What's the matter?" Melissa asked.

"Oh, nothing much. Rudy's stuck in the shower again," Alex answered quickly. "I'll be right back."

Running to the bathroom door, Alex shouted, "Rudy! I'm coming in!" She banged open the door.

"It's too hot! I can't turn it off!" Rudy wailed from behind the shower curtain.

"I'll get it!" Alex shouted to her little brother. She threw him a towel. "Here, wrap up in this."

Rudy wrapped himself in the towel and stepped out of the shower. Alex wrestled with the shower faucet. Water sprayed her hair and face as she whirled the faucet first one direction and then another. It was hard to remember which direction was on and which was off.

Ever since her father had insisted on replacing the leaky shower faucet himself, the family had had problems. The faucet now turned toward "hot" for cold water and "cold" for hot water. Alex's younger brother, Rudy, had the most trouble of all. He always seemed to turn the faucet the wrong way and the water would get so hot that he could not get close enough to turn it off.

"There you go, Goblin," Alex said to her

brother when she had finally turned off the water.

"Thanks, Alex," Rudy mumbled.

"What happened? Where did you go?" Melissa asked as soon as Alex had returned to her bedroom.

"Oh, I had to turn the shower off for Rudy," Alex replied. She flopped down on her bed and smiled at Melissa. Melissa was a new girl at school. At her mother's suggestion, Alex had invited Melissa to spend the night.

"Would you like to play a game?" Alex asked Melissa. "We have lots of board games, or we could play something on the computer."

"No . . . let's sneak out of the house and walk down to the school," Melissa suggested.

Alex looked at Melissa in surprise. "What for?" she asked.

Melissa shrugged. "It's something to do," she replied.

Alex glanced out her window. It was

almost dark. "It's too late. My parents wouldn't want us to do that."

"Of course they wouldn't." Melissa rolled her eyes. "But that's what makes it fun. Besides, they would never know."

"No, we'd better not." Alex shook her head. Her parents had a way of discovering those kinds of things, and Alex did not want to spend the first weekend of fifth grade grounded.

"Okay," sighed Melissa. "Let's go downstairs and hang out with your sister and her friends."

Alex's older sister, Barbara, and a group of her friends were listening to music in the family room.

"Naw," Alex wrinkled her nose. "Barbara wouldn't like having us around."

"So what?" Melissa scowled. "It's your house, too, isn't it?"

"Yeah, but . . ." Alex began.

"Who cares what your sister wants!" Melissa went on.

Alex was getting annoyed with Melissa.

"I care!" she exclaimed. "My sister and I have an agreement. She doesn't bother me when my friends are over, and I don't bother her and her friends."

Melissa just gave Alex a sarcastic smile.

"Uh . . . " Alex was almost afraid to suggest anything else. "Would you want to play Ping-Pong in the basement?"

Melissa sighed in a very bored way.

"Okay!" Alex threw her hands up in the air. "We can just watch television."

"Let's play Ping-Pong," Melissa finally said. "At least then we can walk through the family room on our way to the basement."

Alex shook her head as she followed Melissa down the stairs and through the family room. This evening had not started out well at all.

"It was awful!" Alex told her best friend, Janie, the next day. "All Melissa wanted to do were things that would get me in trouble. And then she'd get mad

11

when I told her we couldn't do those things.

"What's the matter with her?" Janie exclaimed. "Why did she want to get you in trouble?"

"It was like she didn't care," Alex told her friend. "She kept bugging Barbara until Barbara got really mad and told Mom and Mom got mad at me!"

"Oh, no!" Janie cried.

"Oh, it's okay," said Alex. "I explained it all to Mom and Barbara later, and they aren't mad at me anymore."

"That's good," replied Janie.

"There is one good thing about all of this," Alex said with a grin. "Mom doesn't want me to ask Melissa to spend the night again!"

"It's too bad Melissa's in your class at school," Janie observed. Janie and Alex were in different classrooms this year.

"Oh, it's no big deal," Alex replied. "I can just ignore her."

But when Alex got to school on

Monday, she found that she was the one who was ignored. None of the girls in her classroom would speak to her. Whenever Alex tried to start a conversation with them, the girls would walk away. However, Alex noticed that Melissa had no trouble talking to the girls. In fact, she seemed to be the center of their attention.

By lunchtime, Alex was angry and very lonely. Standing by herself in the lunch line, she felt as if she were the only one in the world without a friend.

If only Janie were here, she thought to herself. Why was Janie's class always late for lunch?

"Hel-lo, Al-ex," a sudden voice sang in her ear. It was Melissa. She was carrying a lunch tray. Before Alex knew what was happening, Melissa sprinkled a few peas on Alex's toes. Alex tried to jump out of the way but only managed to squish the peas under her feet.

"A few gross peas for a gross person!" Melissa called over her shoulder. She ran to a table and sat down quickly. Sitting at the table were the girls from Alex's class. They giggled at Melissa's joke.

Alex faced straight ahead in line. She did not look right or left. She ignored the giggles all around her.

Upon getting her lunch tray, Alex carried it to an empty table at the very back of the cafeteria. She sat down facing the wall. She did not want to look at anyone.

Blinking back hot, angry tears, Alex began to choke down her food. Angry, confused thoughts raced through her mind. Why were the girls treating her this way? What had she done? Alex could not think of one single thing that she had done to make them mad at her.

"Alex!" Janie suddenly called out from behind Alex's chair. "What are you doing at this table? I almost couldn't find you!"

She sat down next to Alex. Julie and Lorraine, two other friends, sat across from Alex and Janie.

"I'm surprised you even want to sit at the same table as me!" Alex snapped at her friends.

"Huh? What do you mean?" they asked.

"No one in my whole class wants to sit with me or talk to me," Alex exploded, "except Melissa Howard. She threw peas at my feet and called me gross!"

Janie, Julie, and Lorraine exchanged surprised glances. They listened carefully as Alex told them how the girls in her class would not speak to her.

"That's strange," Janie commented. "I wonder why nobody would talk to you?"

Alex shrugged her shoulders. "I can't think of one single reason."

"Well, it sounds like Melissa Howard is behind it all," declared Janie.

"Yeah," Alex agreed, "but why would she be mean to me? All I did was ask her to spend the night with me. You don't usually get mad at someone for that!"

Janie did not have an answer. Neither did Julie or Lorraine.

"Don't worry, Alex," Julie patted her arm. "We'll figure the whole thing out."

"Yeah, Alex, everything will be okay," Lorraine smiled.

Alex smiled back at her friends. Even if everything else went wrong, she was grateful for her three good friends.

At the last hour of the school day, Alex and several others walked down the hall to the band room. The fifth graders were joining the Kingswood School band for the first time.

Alex was excited. In her right hand she carried a large music case that contained a beautiful, shiny, brass trumpet. She had waited a long time for just such a trumpet, picturing in her mind how it would look when she held it to her lips and blew the most powerful blast of musical notes. And the best part of all was that it was her very own trumpet. Alex had already taken three lessons at the music store. She felt confident in her trumpet-playing ability.

In the band room, Alex hurried to an empty chair between Janie and Lorraine. Julie sat on the other side of Janie.

Janie and Julie each held small music cases on their laps. They were going to play flutes in the band.

"I hope they have enough baritones," Lorraine whispered to Alex. Lorraine wanted to play one of the school's large brass horns called a baritone. Alex thought the baritone would be good for Lorraine. After all, the baritone was big, and so was Lorraine.

Mr. Sharp, the band teacher, brought the class to order. "I want everyone to divide into groups according to your instruments," he said. "I want the drums over there," Mr. Sharp waved his hand in one direction, "and the trumpets and baritones over there," he waved in a different direction, "and the flutes over there. . . ."

Alex was surprised to find that she was the only girl in the middle of a group of

boys. Not one other girl had a trumpet.

Feeling odd and a little outcast, Alex flopped down in a chair at the end of a row. Much to her disgust, Eddie Thompson sat down next to her. Eddie was the class clown and generally caused as much trouble as he could. Lately, he had begun to carry sunflower seeds in his back pocket, shooting them at various targets.

Doing her best to ignore Eddie, Alex opened her trumpet case and pulled out her instrument. She stood it up on the other side of her chair—as far away from Eddie as possible. Then Alex grabbed the mouthpiece and had just started to fit it on to her trumpet when someone called, "Help, Alex, help!"

Alex whirled around. Lorraine sat in the row of chairs behind her. She was slumped over a baritone that sat on the floor. One of her arms seemed to be stuck inside the huge instrument.

"Help, help, it's eating my arm!" Lorraine cried.

Alex leaped off her chair and ran to rescue Lorraine.

"Ha! Ha! Ha!" Lorraine laughed as soon as Alex reached her side. "I was only kidding!" Lorraine easily popped her arm out of the baritone.

"Very funny, Lorraine," Alex chuckled.

Just then, Mr. Sharp called for order in the band room. Alex scurried back to her chair. When she reached it, to her dismay, Eddie Thompson had picked up her trumpet and was fiddling with it.

"Give me my trumpet!" Alex cried and snatched the instrument away from Eddie.

"Okay, okay," Eddie held up his hands. "Don't have a major hissy fit. I was just looking at it."

Alex checked her trumpet over carefully. Everything looked okay. But she was still uneasy. Had Eddie done something to her trumpet?

"We are going to begin learning the notes to a simple song," Mr. Sharp was saying, "but first, can anyone here play the C scale?"

Alex quickly looked up. She had learned to play the C scale in her first music lesson. She raised her hand.

"Okay, Alex," Mr. Sharp nodded. "Show us how the C scale should be played."

Quickly clamping the mouthpiece to her trumpet, Alex stood up and held it to her lips. She paid no attention to the giggling beside her. Let the boys laugh! She'd show them how good a trumpet player she really was.

Taking a deep breath, Alex blew, "BLEEEEEAAAAAHHHHH!" The note immediately went sour. A rattle sounded deep inside the trumpet. Then, try as she might, Alex could get no air to pass through the trumpet. She blew until her face was purple, but no sound came out of the trumpet.

The boys in her section practically rolled off their chairs in laughter. Eddie Thompson laughed the loudest of them all.

"EDDIE THOMPSON!" Alex screamed at the top of her lungs. "WHAT DID YOU DO TO MY TRUMPET?"

And then, because the day had not gone well for Alex and because Eddie grinned at her in such an exasperating way, Alex gave in to her angry feelings. SMACK! She whacked Eddie on top of his head with her music book.

Stunned silence filled the band room.

CHAPTER 2

Ugly Gossip

"Owwwwwwwww!" moaned Eddie Thompson. He rubbed the top of his head where Alex had hit him.

"Alex, would you and Eddie like to explain what is going on between the two of you?" asked Mr. Sharp. He folded his arms across his chest and tapped his foot.

"Eddie did something horrible to my trumpet and now it won't play," Alex told her teacher. She demonstrated her point by once again blowing on her trumpet's mouthpiece. No sound came out.

Mr. Sharp replaced Alex's mouthpiece with his own and tried to play her trumpet. He could not get it to play either. He held it up to his ear and gently shook it. A faint rattle could be heard.

"Did you put something inside this instrument?" Mr. Sharp asked Eddie.

"Uh, well, I guess so," Eddie smiled sheepishly at the teacher. The other boys laughed.

"This is not funny!" Mr. Sharp told the boys with a frown. "If you cannot treat musical instruments with respect, there is no room for you in the band." He glared at Eddie. "You may sit in the time-out chair for the rest of the period."

"But what about Alex?" Eddie complained as he shuffled his way to the chair.

"Hmmmpf!" snorted Mr. Sharp. "If you had messed with one of my instruments, I might have hit you with something harder than a softcover music book!"

The class laughed. Eddie sat down in the time-out chair.

Mr. Sharp showed Alex how to flush out her trumpet with water at the sink in the back of the classroom. She watched carefully as Mr. Sharp took off the mouthpiece and pulled the tuning slide out of its place. He then ran a stream of water through the trumpet.

Almost immediately, two tiny objects floated out of the end of the instrument. Alex picked them up.

"Sunflower seeds!" she cried in a disgusted voice.

Mr. Sharp made Eddie empty his pockets of sunflower seeds. Alex returned to her seat with her newly restored trumpet. If this was how band class began, she was almost afraid to think about the rest of the year.

"The girls won't talk to *me* either!" Janie complained as she hurried down the sidewalk toward Alex.

Janie had stopped after school to ask Melissa and the other girls why they were not speaking to Alex.

Alex had waited for Janie outside. She frowned at Janie's report. "Why won't they talk to you?"

"Melissa says that no one can talk to

me because I'm your best friend!" Janie replied, coming to stand beside Alex.

"But I still don't know why they aren't speaking to me!" Alex exclaimed in frustration.

"I know," Janie shrugged her shoulders, "and we can't find out until they decide to talk to one of us again."

Alex stomped her foot angrily. "THIS IS RIDICULOUS! I HAVE DONE NOTHING WRONG TO ANY OF THOSE GIRLS!" she shouted.

"Come on, Alex," Janie said. She began pulling Alex down the sidewalk. Other children stared at Alex, surprised at her angry outburst.

"NERDS! THEY'RE ALL NERDS!" Alex shouted one more time. She angrily stomped down the sidewalk.

On reaching home, Alex said good-bye to Janie and rushed inside. She wanted to talk to her mother. She found Mother in the backyard, the garden hose in her hand, standing by a very wet and unhappy-looking black dog. Mother's clothes were splotched with paint.

"What are you doing?" Alex asked.

"I'm giving T-Bone a bath," Mother answered. "He's been a very bad dog today."

"What did he do?" Alex wanted to know.

"Well, I was doing some painting in the basement," Mother explained, "and T-Bone sat down in the pan of paint."

"Oh, no!" Alex began to giggle.

"That's not all," Mother told her. "When he sat down, the paint pan flipped in the air. The paint splattered everywhere, but most of it landed on T-Bone's back!"

"Oh, poor T-Bone!" Alex laughed. She grabbed the soapy brush and began to scrub T-Bone's paint-splattered tail. While she worked, she told Mother about her problems with Melissa Howard and the girls in her class.

"Do you mean that *none* of the girls would speak to you?" Mother raised her eyebrows in surprise.

"The only girls in the fifth grade that would speak to me were Janie, Julie, and Lorraine," Alex replied, a disgusted look on her face.

"That's the silliest thing I have ever heard," declared Mother.

"Yeah, and it looks like Melissa Howard started it all," said Alex.

"Hmmmm." Mother thought for a moment. "You and Melissa didn't get along too well when she spent the night with you, but I didn't think you did anything to make her want to turn all the girls against you."

"I didn't do anything bad to her," Alex said. "So now, for no reason at all, Melissa's made up some stupid story about me and all the girls believe it." Alex stamped her foot. "They look at me and giggle and whisper to each other." To her dismay, Alex felt the tears gather in the corners of her eyes.

"Oh, honey, I'm sorry," said Mother. She put a wet, soapy arm around Alex.

"It's just not fair," Alex sobbed into her mother's shoulder. "I have been friends with those girls a lot longer than Melissa Howard. Why would they listen to her?"

"Oh, because she's filled their ears with some kind of juicy gossip about you," Mother replied.

"Juicy gossip?" Alex frowned. "I thought gossip was only for old ladies."

Mother laughed. "Oh, no, Alex, anybody can gossip. All you need is one person who wants to spread ugly, nasty rumors about someone else."

"But why would anyone want to do that?" Alex persisted.

"Because some people think that it's fun to gossip," Mother answered.

"That's sick!" exclaimed Alex.

"Yes, gossip is very 'sick,' as you say, and hurts a lot of people," said Mother.

"But what ugly rumors would Melissa want to spread about me?" Alex wondered.

"Why don't you call her and ask her?" Mother suggested.

"You mean call her on the telephone?" Alex's eyes opened wide at the idea.

"Sure, why not give it a try?" asked Mother. "Maybe she'll talk to you on the telephone and you can find out just what is going on."

"Great idea!" Alex threw the soapy brush to her mother and began to run across the backyard.

"Alex!" Mother called after her. "Where are you going?"

"Over to Janie's house!" Alex called

back. "I'm gonna get Janie to help me call Melissa!"

Alex was in such a hurry that she leaped over the fence that separated her backyard from Janie's backyard.

"JANIE! JANIE, ARE YOU THERE?" Alex bellowed through the screen door at the back of Janie's house.

"Why, hello, Alex," said Mrs. Edwards, Janie's mother. She opened the door for Alex. "Janie's in the kitchen."

Alex thanked Mrs. Edwards and hurried to the kitchen. She found Janie perched on a stool at a counter, busily shoving handfuls of tiny objects into her mouth.

"Are those sunflower seeds?" Alex demanded with her hands on her hips.

"Alex!" Janie exclaimed. "Where'd you come from?"

"Never mind! Are those sunflower seeds?" Alex repeated.

"Yes," Janie sighed.

"Janie! How could you eat sunflower

seeds after all the trouble those things have caused me today?" asked Alex.

"Sorry!"

"Come on, we've got a job to do," Alex dragged Janie off of her stool. "You gotta help me call Melissa Howard."

"What?" Janie stared at Alex in surprise. "Why?"

"Because I need to try and stop all the gossip," Alex answered.

"Gossip?" Janie echoed.

"Yeah, gossip! That's what you call it when people talk about you behind your back," Alex explained. "And I gotta find out what Melissa is saying that makes everyone not want to talk to me."

"Okay, let's do it," Janie agreed. She got out the Kingswood Elementary School telephone directory and handed it to Alex.

Alex dialed Melissa Howard's number. "Hello, Melissa, this is Alex Brackenbury—"

"Click!" The phone went dead. Alex pushed the receiver button up and down. The dial tone suddenly buzzed in her ear.

"That's funny," Alex said to Janie. "We must have got a bad connection. I'll call again."

"Hello, Melissa," she said after dialing the number once more, "this is Alex."

"I'm not speaking to you," hissed the voice on the other end of the line. "Click!" The phone went dead again.

"Brussels sprouts! She hung up on me!" Alex exclaimed. She banged down the receiver and stomped around the kitchen.

"Here, let me try," said Janie. She dialed Melissa's number.

"Hello, Melissa, this is Janie Edwards," Janie said into the receiver. "I would like to know why you aren't speaking to Alex."

Janie was silent for a moment as she listened to Melissa. "But can't you just tell me why . . ." Janie began.

There was silence. Then, suddenly, Janie slammed down the receiver. She, too, stomped around the kitchen. "She said she can't tell me anything because she's not speaking to me either!"

"But how are we ever going to find out what gossip Melissa is spreading around?" Alex wailed.

Janie looked at her friend sadly. "I don't know," she admitted.

"I suppose Melissa is laughing at us right now!" Alex fumed.

"Yeah and I suppose she's telling all of her friends how she wouldn't speak to us even on the telephone," added Janie.

"They used to be *our* friends," Alex reminded Janie.

The girls sank down on two of the stools at the kitchen counter. Janie held her head in her hands. Alex drummed the countertop with her fingers.

"Hey!" Alex cried suddenly. "I almost forgot! Julie was going to try and walk home with Melissa today. Let's see if she learned anything."

"Good idea," Janie reached for the telephone. "I'll call her."

"I'll get on the other phone," Alex called and ran into the next room. She picked up the receiver just as Julie answered on the other end.

"Hello, Julie, this is Janie."

"And Alex," added Alex from her phone.

"Oh, hi . . ." said Julie in what Alex thought was a rather unfriendly voice.

Janie didn't seem to notice. She told Julie how she and Alex had called Melissa and how Melissa would not talk to either of them.

"So we were wondering, were you able to find out anything from Melissa?" Janie asked Julie.

"Uh . . ." Julie hesitated. "Can I call you back later? I can't talk right now. My mom needs me."

"Oh, sure," Janie replied.

"Did Julie sound funny to you?" Alex asked when she had returned to the kitchen.

"Maybe a little," Janie answered. "She must have been busy with something."

"Maybe she really didn't want to talk to

us," Alex said, worried. "Maybe *she* has decided not to speak to us either!"

"Don't be ridiculous! Julie's our friend. She's not like the other girls."

"I guess you're right." Alex tried to smile. "I'm getting too worried about everything."

"Right! Loosen up!" Janie laughed. "Everything will be all right." She passed a package toward Alex. "Here, have some sunflower seeds!"

"Okay," Alex giggled, dumping a bunch of the seeds into her hand. "I oughta learn how to shoot these seeds so I can defend myself against Eddie Thompson."

Janie grabbed a pack of straws and she and Alex spent the rest of the afternoon learning to shoot sunflower seeds.

CHAPTER 3

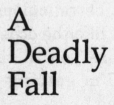

A Deadly Fall

The next day at school was absolutely awful. Just as Alex suspected, the girls in her class knew that she and Janie had tried to call Melissa the night before.

Alex's ears burned and her face turned red as she heard her name spoken again and again by the circle of girls at the back of the classroom.

"So she called Melissa last night," said a sarcastic voice.

"How dare she?" cried another voice.

"Doesn't she know we're not speaking to her?" a third, more nasty-sounding voice asked as they all giggled.

Alex slumped down in her seat. She noticed that a few boys were listening to

36

what the girls were saying. If the boys found out that the girls were not speaking to her, Alex would be horribly teased.

Fortunately for Alex, Mrs. Hibbits, her teacher, called for silence. Everyone had to sit down and class began.

As the morning wore on, things did not improve for Alex. She tried not to notice the cruel stares from the girls. Every time anyone whispered or giggled, Alex was sure the joke was on her.

By the time lunch rolled around, Alex was extremely upset. She waited impatiently for Janie and Lorraine and Julie to join her at the lonely end of the last cafeteria table.

"I'm so glad you're here," she cried in relief as Janie and Lorraine sat down on either side of her. Alex looked around.

"Where's Julie?" Alex asked Lorraine.

"Uh . . ." Lorraine hesitated and looked helplessly at Janie.

"She's over there!" Janie said angrily and pointed at a crowded table.

"WHAT!" Alex shouted. "YOU MEAN SHE . . . YOU MEAN SHE'S JOINED THAT GROUP?" Alex jumped up and loudly banged both hands on the table.

"Calm down, Alex," Janie hissed. "It's not going to help to scream about it. You'll only get in trouble."

"But . . . but . . . "Alex slowly sat down again. "I told you Julie sounded funny on the phone yesterday!"

"Yeah," replied Janie. "I guess you were right about her. I didn't think Julie would do such a thing!"

"Neither did I," sighed Alex.

That afternoon, Alex and Janie trudged up the steep Juniper Street hill on their way home from school. Ahead of them walked Alex's younger brother, Rudy, and his best friend, Jason.

The girls were silent. Each was thinking her own thoughts. Suddenly, Rudy buzzed a giant, blue plastic airplane in front of Alex's face.

"Goblin!" Alex cried, using her special nickname for her brother. "Cut it out!"

"Grouchhead!" Rudy called, sticking his tongue out at Alex. He and Jason skipped up the street ahead of the girls.

Alex sighed and looked at Janie. "I guess I have been sort of a grouch lately. It's just that everything at school has been going wrong."

"I know," Janie sympathized.

"I wanted things to go right, especially at the beginning of fifth grade."

"Yeah," Janie nodded her head. "Fifth grade shouldn't be like this. It should be, well, sort of grown up."

As the girls talked, they continued walking up the hill. They were so busy speaking to one another that they did not notice Rudy high up in a tree until he and Jason hollered down at them.

Looking up, Alex gasped. Rudy was in a very dangerous position. He had climbed up a monstrous old tree that grew beside the sidewalk and had crawled

along a fat limb that stuck out over the sidewalk. Apparently he had stopped his climb, too afraid to move out farther onto the limb and too afraid to inch his way backwards to the trunk. He had wrapped himself around the fat old limb and was holding on tight.

"BRUSSELS SPROUTS, GOBLIN!" Alex cupped her hands around her mouth and yelled her loudest. "GET DOWN FROM THERE BEFORE YOU KILL YOURSELF!"

"I CAN'T GET DOWN!" Rudy wailed.

"I TOLD HIM NOT TO GO OUT ON THAT LIMB," Jason called down to Alex. Jason was perched much lower in the tree than Rudy.

"WELL, WHAT'D HE GO OUT THERE FOR ANYWAY?" Alex asked Jason.

"TO GET HIS BLUE BOMBER!" Jason pointed to a spot near Rudy.

Alex squinted. There, close to where Rudy clung for dear life, was the tail end of the blue plastic airplane.

"Oh, brussels sprouts!" Alex sighed. "I suppose I have to go up and get him."

"Be careful, Alex," Janie warned. Janie was afraid to climb trees and did not like to watch other people do it.

Alex, however, loved to climb trees and for quite a while had had her eye on this particular tree. Its owner, however, was Mrs. Rudford, who, like Janie, was very nervous about children climbing trees. She had repeatedly told the neighborhood children that they were not to climb the trees in her yard.

Alex grinned as she scooted up the trunk of the tree. If Mrs. Rudford caught her climbing the tree, she would just say that she was trying to rescue her brother.

Quickly passing Jason, Alex pulled herself up alongside Rudy's limb. She could see why her brother was afraid to move. The wind was blowing hard at the top of the tree. The branches swayed back and forth. Even with Rudy on it, the fat old limb moved up and down in the wind.

"Okay, Goblin, you're gonna have to move back toward the trunk," Alex said. She was as close as she could get to Rudy without actually climbing onto the limb herself.

"I can't!" Rudy cried.

"You have to! There's no other way," Alex told her brother. "Just scoot backwards, a little at a time."

Rudy hesitated for a few moments, then, at Alex's insistence, he began inching his way back to the tree trunk.

"You're doing great, Goblin. You only have a little ways to go."

Just as Rudy got to where Alex could almost grab his foot, Mrs. Rudford stepped out on her front porch. She immediately spotted Alex and Rudy high up in her tree. Mrs. Rudford threw her hands in the air and screamed at the top of her lungs, "AHHHHHIIIIIEEEEEE!"

The cry was so unexpected and so loud that it badly frightened the children. Alex felt her heart jump in terror and only just

43

managed to grab hold of the trunk to keep herself from falling.

Rudy did not have anything to grab, and already being terribly frightened of falling, lost his balance and rolled off of the limb. With a screech, he fell to the ground far below!

Alex screamed as she watched her brother hit the ground hard and then lie very still. He lay in a crumpled position. One of his arms was bent funny with the elbow pointing straight up at Alex.

"Why doesn't he move?" Alex asked herself. "Why doesn't he cry?" She waited for Rudy's shout of pain, but it didn't come. Everything was deathly quiet.

Alex forced her legs and arms to climb down the tree's trunk. As she neared the ground, she could see that Rudy's eyes were closed.

"He's not even awake!" she told herself. His face looked as white as a sheet. Was he breathing? Was he still alive?

CHAPTER 4

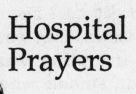

Hospital Prayers

"CALL THE POLICE! CALL THE AMBULANCE! OH, CALL SOMEBODY!" Mrs. Rudford ran about the yard shouting at the top of her voice.

Another time, Alex might have laughed at Mrs. Rudford's behavior. But right now, Alex was too worried about Rudy to laugh at anything.

"Rudy! Rudy! Can you hear me?" Alex called to her brother.

Rudy made no response. His face was so white. He made no movement whatsoever. Alex fought the fear that steadily rose in her throat. She forced herself to think.

What should she do? She needed a

grown-up. Mrs. Rudford was no help. She needed her mother. Should she run up the street to get her? No, she couldn't leave Rudy. Besides, that would take too much time. Her brother was badly hurt and needed an ambulance right away. There was no one else to do it. *She* would have to call an ambulance.

"Janie!" Alex shouted to her friend. "Go get my mom! Quick!" She watched as her best friend started up the street as fast as she could go.

"Jason, stay here with Rudy!" Alex commanded the younger boy. She trotted toward Mrs. Rudford's front door.

"Where are you going?" Jason shouted.

"I'm gonna call an ambulance!" Alex called over her shoulder.

Alex rushed into the house. She found the telephone in the kitchen. Taking a deep breath, Alex dialed the emergency number, 911. She had never dialed 911 before. She was nervous and terribly frightened.

"911–EMERGENCY!" a deep voice boomed on the other end of the line.

"Uh, hello?" said Alex. "I have an emergency."

"What kind of emergency, honey?" Immediately the deep voice softened.

"My brother fell out of a tree and he's hurt bad," Alex answered.

"Hold on," the voice responded. "I am transferring you to the ambulance dispatcher."

Alex heard a click on the line and then a lady's voice said, "Fire and Ambulance! Where do you need us?"

"Oh!" Alex wailed. "I don't know the address! I mean, I'm at a neighbor's house. It's on Juniper Street."

"The address has flashed on my screen," the woman told her. "Do you need an ambulance?"

"Oh, yes, please hurry!" Alex shouted. "My brother needs help!"

"The ambulance is on its way," replied the woman in a soothing tone. "What happened to your brother?"

"He fell out of a tree. It's a really big tree and he's just lying on the ground sorta crumpled up and he won't move or say anything." Alex's voice shook and hot tears began to sting her eyes.

"Is your brother unconscious?" the woman asked.

"Yes," Alex sniffed. She burst into tears and could not answer any more questions for a moment.

"How old is your brother?" the woman asked gently.

"He's eight years old," Alex finally managed to answer.

"And how old are you?"

"I'm ten."

"Is there an adult with you?" the woman asked.

"No," Alex answered. She did not count Mrs. Rudford. "But my best friend went to get my mother."

"Good," replied the woman. "Here's what I want you to do. Go back outside and stay with your brother until the ambulance comes. Can you do that?"

"Yes," Alex replied. She hung up the phone and wiped her eyes on her shirtsleeve.

Stepping outside, Alex breathed a sigh of relief. Both her mother and her older sister, Barbara, were there. They were bent over Rudy.

"I'm so glad you're here!" Alex shouted as she ran to them.

Mother looked up at Alex. She wore an anxious look. "Did you call an ambulance?" she asked.

"Yes, it should be here right away," Alex replied.

"Thank you, honey," said Mother. She grabbed Alex's hand and Barbara's hand and the three of them knelt beside Rudy.

"Please, Lord God," Mother prayed out loud. "Place Your loving hand on Rudy. Heal his injuries and restore him to us. In the name of Jesus, we pray."

At that moment, the ambulance

arrived. Its lights whirled and flashed. Alex could not help but think how excited Rudy would have been to see an ambulance in his neighborhood. If only he could see it. If only he wasn't hurt.

Two young men leaped from the ambulance and ran into the yard carrying a stretcher. In a few moments, they had loaded Rudy onto the stretcher and lifted him into the back of the ambulance.

Alex waved good-bye to Janie and Jason as she climbed into the ambulance with her mother and Barbara to ride to the hospital with Rudy.

Mother never stopped praying the entire way to the hospital. Alex prayed too. Over and over she whispered, "Help Rudy, Lord Jesus, help Rudy!"

When they reached the hospital, they were met by several people in white uniforms. Rudy was whisked inside. Mother followed the stretcher into a room. Barbara went to call Father. Alex was left to sit alone in the waiting room.

It wasn't long before tears began to slide down Alex's face. Sure, Rudy could be a pest sometimes and an absolute brat at other times. But all and all, he was a pretty good little brother, and Alex wanted to keep him.

"Oh, Barbara!" Alex cried as soon as her sister returned. "What if Rudy doesn't make it?"

Barbara sat down on the sofa next to Alex and hugged her younger sister. "He will make it," Barbara whispered. "I'm sure he'll be all right."

"But what if he's bleeding inside or what if he hurt his head really bad or what if—" worried Alex.

Barbara grabbed Alex's shoulders and looked straight into her eyes. "We have to trust God that none of those things have happened to Rudy," Barbara said firmly. "We have to believe that God is taking care of him, okay?"

Alex nodded, "Okay."

Suddenly, a tall, dark-haired man

burst though the door. He rushed over to Barbara and Alex.

"Dad!" Alex cried in surprise. Her father, normally so jolly, wore such a worried expression on his face that she had hardly recognized him.

"I came as quickly as I could," gasped Father. "Where's your mother and Rudy?"

"In that room." Alex and Barbara pointed to a set of double doors across the hallway.

At that moment, a nurse came up to Father. "Are you Mr. Brackenbury?" she asked.

"Yes," he answered.

"Please come with me," the nurse said. Father gave Alex and Barbara a weak smile and turned to follow the nurse.

"Wait, Dad!" Alex cried and ran to him. Taking his hand in hers, she told him, "Don't worry. I know the Lord will take care of Rudy."

A smile flickered across her father's face. "Thank you, Firecracker," he said, using his special nickname for Alex. "I needed to hear that."

It wasn't too long after Father left that Mother appeared. She was smiling and had good news. "Your brother does have a broken arm," she reported, "but the doctors can find nothing else wrong with him."

"Hurray!" Alex cried.

"Well, that's an answer to our prayers," Barbara exclaimed.

"I think you're right." Mother smiled. "The doctors said it was a miracle that Rudy wasn't seriously injured from such a high fall."

"Yeah, that was a long drop," Alex agreed. "I'll never forget how he looked lying unconscious under that tree." Alex's voice suddenly cracked with emotion.

"When I first saw him, I was so scared that I almost got sick," Barbara admitted.

"I know," Mother whispered. Tears slid down their faces as they hugged one another tightly.

Before they could dry their eyes, Father joined them in the waiting room. He no longer looked worried. Instead, he wore a happy smile.

"Firecracker," he said to Alex, "I hear you called the ambulance. That was a very brave thing to do."

"Thanks, Dad," replied Alex. She wriggled into her father's arms.

"By the way, your brother wants to see you," Father said to Alex.

"Me? He wants to see me?" Alex asked.

"Yes, he said something about a Blue Bomber," Father chuckled.

"Oh, no!" Alex exclaimed. "If he thinks I'm gonna go back up that tree to get his dumb airplane, he's crazy!"

Her family laughed. They walked, arm in arm, down the hallway to the hospital room where Rudy was resting.

Alex stared at her brother. He looked awfully small lying on such a high hospital bed. His face was still pale, but not as white as before.

"Hi, Goblin," Alex said as she stepped up beside the bed.

"Alex!" Rudy's eyes lit up when he saw her. "You gotta go rescue my Blue Bomber outa the tree."

"No!" Mother put a stop to it. "No one in this family is climbing that tree again!"

"I'm afraid, Rudy," chuckled Father, "that your Blue Bomber has become a permanent addition to Mrs. Rudford's tree."

Everyone laughed. Rudy let them admire the cast on his arm. It completely covered his left arm, running all the way from just under his shoulder to his wrist.

Soon, Alex, Barbara, and Mother got ready to go home. Father was going to stay with Rudy for a while. Then later, Mother would return to the hospital to spend the night with Rudy. The doctors wanted to keep Rudy overnight to make sure that he was all right.

"Bye, Goblin, see you tomorrow," Alex waved to her brother.

It was dark outside. Alex followed her mother and sister through the parking lot to where Father had parked his car. She breathed the cool night air and sighed in relief. Everything had turned out well. Rudy would be all right.

"Thank You, Lord Jesus," Alex whispered, looking at the bright, starry sky. "Thank You for saving Rudy."

CHAPTER 5

A Bathroom Fight

"Alex! Be careful!" Janie gasped, catching the giant punch bowl a second before it sailed off the end of the table.

Alex, while pulling a box of cookies out from underneath the table, had tried to stand up too soon and bumped the table, sending the punch bowl flying. Only Janie's quick move had saved the girls from disaster.

"Brussels sprouts! I just know something horrible is going to happen before the night is over," Alex worried. "I wish Mrs. Hibbits had never picked us to serve the cookies and punch at Back to School Night."

"Now, Alex," Janie scolded. "It's supposed to be an honor to serve the refreshments at Back to School Night."

"Well, it's not gonna be much of an honor if the punch bowl crashes to the floor and breaks into a hundred million pieces." Alex scowled. "I've almost knocked it off the table twice!"

"Just be more careful when you fill the cookie tray," replied Janie. She poked Alex in the ribs and smiled sweetly at a family with two young children approaching the refreshment table.

The mother of the two children picked up a glass of punch. She handed it to the small boy.

"I don't like this punch!" the boy cried after taking a small sip.

"MINE!" his little sister shouted and knocked the cup from his hand. The glass of punch splattered to the floor and left a bright, red puddle on the shiny gymnasium floor.

"OH, NO!" Janie and Alex wailed. They

rushed to wipe up the mess, but they did not get it cleaned up before Mrs. Larson, the school principal, saw it.

"GET THAT PUNCH OFF THE GYM FLOOR!" Mrs. Larson demanded, hurrying over to them. Her voice rang through the gymnasium, grabbing the attention of everyone in the room. People suddenly stopped their conversations to stare at Alex, Janie, and the spilled punch.

With the principal's help, the girls got the punch cleaned off the floor, but it was still sticky to the touch.

"Alex, go get some wet paper towels from the bathroom," directed Mrs. Larson.

Hurrying as fast as she could through the crowded hallways, Alex burst through the door of the nearest girls' bathroom. What she saw made her wish she had picked another bathroom—any other bathroom.

Right in front of Alex stood Melissa Howard and her best friend, Crystal

Dixon! They stared at her with fierce, frowning faces.

Alex was so surprised that, for a few moments, she could not speak. She stared back at the two girls. Dimly, she became aware of the sound of running water. Peering around Melissa and Crystal, Alex saw that the sinks in the bathroom were clogged with paper towels and water was pouring over their sides and onto the floor. Melissa and Crystal were flooding the bathroom deliberately!

"TURN OFF THE WATER!" Alex shouted at Melissa.

"NO!" Melissa shouted back.

"MAKE US!" taunted Crystal.

As Alex tried to move to the sinks, Crystal and Melissa blocked her way. "YOU'RE MAKING A MESS!" Alex cried.

"So what?" answered Melissa.

Alex could see that talking was getting her nowhere fast. All of a sudden, she lunged forward, faked to the left, and moved to the right. It was a good soccer fake and she had used it many times on the field.

The fake completely fooled Melissa and Crystal. Before they could recover, Alex had reached one of the sinks and had turned off the water.

"LEAVE THE SINKS ALONE!" Melissa cried and called Alex a bad name. She rushed at Alex with her fists flying.

Alex took aim and swung her fist as hard as she could at Melissa's chin. POW! Melissa fell backwards onto the wet floor. Alex then turned toward Crystal. Crystal backed away. She grabbed Melissa and the two girls fled out the door.

Breathing deeply, Alex tried to control the anger that burned inside of her. Her arms and legs shook. She moved unsteadily from sink to sink, turning off all of the faucets.

Just as she shut the last faucet off, the door opened and in walked Mrs. Larson. "Alex, why is it taking you so long to get the paper . . ."

The last words died on the principal's lips as she stared in disbelief at the water disaster.

"WHAT IS GOING ON HERE?" she demanded. The frown on her face looked absolutely frightening.

"I didn't do it," Alex squeaked as she stood on her wobbly legs and endured the principal's angry stare. Alex was so upset that her stomach seemed to flip-flop. She sank down on the floor, not caring that it was covered with water.

"Oh, Alex, I am sorry," Mrs. Larson said, squatting down beside her. "I didn't mean to accuse you. Besides," she said rubbing her chin in an attitude of deep thought, "now that I think about it, I know who did it."

"You do?" Alex asked surprised.

"I believe so," answered the principal. "I saw Melissa Howard and Crystal Dixon just before I walked in here. Both girls looked terribly upset, and Melissa's dress was wet. I wondered what they were up to. They are the ones who caused this mess, aren't they?"

Alex nodded and sighed in relief. It was good that Mrs. Larson knew the truth, and the best part about it was that Alex had not had to tell on Melissa and Crystal.

"Come on, Alex." Mrs. Larson helped Alex to stand. "We need to get you out of here. Oh! Look at the back of your dress. It's sopping wet."

"Oh, that's okay," Alex replied. "It's just

a dumb old dress."

Mrs. Larson chuckled. "It's nice to see you in a dress for a change, Alex."

Alex wrinkled her nose in disgust. She did not like wearing dresses. They were uncomfortable, and she couldn't pitch a softball or dribble a soccer ball in a dress!

When Alex returned to the gym, she found her mother helping Janie serve the punch and cookies.

"What happened to your dress?" Mother asked as soon as she saw Alex.

Alex told Mother and Janie all that had happened. Mother put her arms around Alex. "I'm sorry," she said. "I'll go get your father. We need to get you home and out of that wet dress."

"Sorry I have to leave," Alex apologized to Janie.

"Oh, that's okay," Janie replied. "You know, Alex, you were right about one thing."

"What's that?" Alex asked.

"You were right when you said

something horrible was going to happen tonight," Janie reminded her.

"Oh, yeah," Alex agreed, "I guess it happened."

When Alex got home, she went immediately to her room and changed clothes. After a few minutes, Mother knocked on her door.

"Come in," Alex called.

"I thought you might like some company," Mother said, opening the door. "You just went through a pretty rough time tonight."

"You can say that again," replied Alex. She sat on her bed with her chin in her hands. "I just don't understand why all this bad stuff has to happen to me!" she complained. "I don't know why Melissa was so mad at me in the first place and why none of the other girls would talk to me. It's so unfair!"

"Gossip is a terrible thing," said Mother. She slipped her arm around

Alex's shoulders. "I think the hurts that people give to each other with their tongues do far more damage than the hurts they give each other with their fists."

"So do I," Alex nodded. "You kind of forget about how much it hurts when somebody hits you. But, when somebody says something mean about you, the words stay in your memory for always. I don't think you ever really forget them."

"You're so right," Mother agreed. "Did you know the Bible says that we corrupt our whole bodies when we say something bad?"

"We do?" Alex asked, surprised.

"The apostle James said that just as a small bit in a horse's mouth can direct such a large animal or as a small rudder can turn a big ship, so our small tongues can turn our bodies to good or to evil depending on what we say."

"Wow!" Alex exclaimed. "I knew that if I said something mean about some-one else it would hurt them, but I didn't know that it would hurt me, ιc

"Oh, yes," Mother nodded. "Gc
like poison. You need only a small amou
to do serious harm."

"Brussels sprouts! Melissa Howard
must be full of poison!" Alex exclaimed.

"I'm afraid Melissa and the other girls
don't realize how much they are hurting
themselves by spreading gossip," said
Mother sadly.

"But once gossip gets started, how do
you stop it?" Alex wanted to know.

"Well, the best way to stop gossip is to
refuse to listen to it," replied Mother. "If
people wouldn't listen to gossip, then
there would be no way to pass it on."

"The girls in my class have already
listened to gossip about me," said Alex.
"Even my good friend Julie."

"Do you know what they are saying
about you?" Mother asked.

"No!" Alex crossed her arms over her
chest and frowned. "No one will speak to
me, so I can't find out what they're saying."

"Oh, dear," sighed Mother. "That is a bad situation. I don't see how you can prove that the gossip is wrong unless you know what it is."

"Right, and after tonight, Melissa will be so mad at me that she'll probably spread even more gossip," worried Alex. "Melissa and Crystal will think that I spoiled their fun and that it was my fault Mrs. Larson found out who did it. And then I'm in big trouble! I might as well change schools or something."

"Oh, Alex," Mother cried. "It won't be that bad, will it?"

"No," said Alex grimly. "It will be worse!"

CHAPTER 6

Adventure with T-Bone

When Alex got to school the next day, she found a note inside her desk. The note said, "If you tell on us, you are dead meat!" Small drops of blood dripped from each letter.

The note had to be from Melissa and Crystal. Throwing it back in her desk, Alex stared straight ahead. She pretended not to notice the mean looks from Melissa and Crystal. Let them think what they wanted. She had not been a tattletale. Mrs. Larson had figured out by herself who had messed up the bathroom.

Alex tried to concentrate on Mrs. Hibbits's geography lesson. She could feel the girls' eyes staring at her back.

Mrs. Hibbits was just winding up her

lesson when a commanding figure stepped into the classroom. It was Mrs. Larson and she was not smiling. She whispered something to Mrs. Hibbits.

"Melissa Howard and Crystal Dixon," Mrs. Hibbits called. "You are to go with Mrs. Larson at once."

Melissa shot an angry look at Alex before following the principal out of the door. When Crystal got up, she glared at Alex all the way out of the classroom.

Alex felt her cheeks grow hot. She knew everyone in the classroom was staring at her.

Quickly, Alex bent over her geography book. Hot tears sprang to her eyes. It wasn't fair! She had done nothing wrong, and yet, *she* was getting mean looks.

By morning recess, Melissa and Crystal still had not returned to class. They had not returned by lunchtime. After lunch, during afternoon recess, Alex, Janie, and Lorraine sat on the swings and discussed the matter.

"Why would Mrs. Larson keep Melissa and Crystal in her office this long?" Alex worried.

"Alex! Stop worrying!" Janie ordered. "You did not do anything wrong. It was Melissa and Crystal who flooded the bathroom."

"That's easy for you to say," Alex retorted. "You didn't get the note about being 'DEAD MEAT'!"

"I have a feeling we might all be dead meat real soon," Lorraine suddenly said. "LOOK!" She pointed at a large group of girls marching across the playground and heading straight for Alex and her friends.

"OH, NO!" Janie shouted.

"RUN!" cried Lorraine.

"NO!" Alex held up her hand. "We will not run away! Like Janie says, we have done nothing wrong."

The three girls sat on the swings and nervously waited for the group of girls to reach them. It took all of Alex's willpower to force herself to sit quietly and wait when she really wanted to get up and run.

The girls soon surrounded Alex, Janie, and Lorraine. They all looked angry.

"What happened to Melissa and Crystal?" one of the girls demanded.

"How should I know?" Alex shrugged.

"We think you know," another girl said gruffly. "They gave you some awful looks before they left the room."

"Yeah, maybe it was your fault that they were getting in trouble," added another girl.

"It was not my fault!" Alex shouted. "I did nothing to them."

"That's right!" hollered Janie, who could no longer keep still. "Melissa and Crystal got themselves in trouble!"

"Oh, yeah?" one girl sneered. "And how did they do that?"

Janie and Alex looked at each other. "I guess we might as well tell you," Alex finally said. "Nobody said we shouldn't."

Alex told the girls how she had caught Melissa and Crystal stopping up the sinks and how Mrs. Larson had guessed who had done it.

When Alex finished, most of the girls were frowning. "Why would anyone want to flood a bathroom?" one of them asked.

"No wonder Mrs. Larson was so mad," said someone else.

The group of girls left the swing area, chatting among themselves. Alex, Janie, and Lorraine were alone once again.

"Brussels sprouts!" Alex exclaimed. "I'm glad that's over."

"Me, too," Lorraine agreed. "But did you notice that the girls sounded disgusted at what Melissa and Crystal did?"

"Maybe they'll decide that Melissa is not such a great person after all," Janie added.

"Maybe." Alex's face brightened. "But one good thing has happened for sure. The girls actually spoke to me for the first time all week!"

Janie and Lorraine laughed.

"Did you hear the news?" Janie called to Alex and Lorraine as she ran to meet them after school.

"You mean the news about Melissa and Crystal?" Alex asked.

"Yeah, they are suspended for two days!" Janie exclaimed.

"I know," Alex replied. "That's what everybody's talking about."

"Well, don't you think that's great?" Janie asked. "Now you don't have to see Melissa for two whole days, and maybe you can get to be friends again with the other girls before she comes back."

"Right!" agreed Lorraine. "Then Melissa couldn't do anything about it."

"Sounds good to me!" Alex laughed, leading the way down the sidewalk, across the street, and up the Juniper Street hill. "Why do you think Melissa is so mean?" Alex asked.

"Some kids are mean because their parents are mean to them," Janie replied.

"Or, because they are left alone a lot,"

added Lorraine. She was spending the afternoon with Alex and Janie.

"I wonder where Melissa lives," said Alex.

"We could look up her address in the school directory," Janie suggested.

"Let's do it!" agreed Alex. The girls ran the rest of the way to Alex's house.

Bursting through the front door, Alex led the way to the kitchen. "Hi, Mom!" she called. "We're going to look up Melissa's address in the school directory."

"Whatever for?" Mother asked.

"Oh, we were just wondering where she lives," Alex answered.

Mother shook her head as she set a plate of cookies out on the table.

"Here's her address," Alex announced. She picked up a cookie. "It's 6814 Locust," she said between bites.

"Locust?" Janie repeated. "I wonder where that is?"

"It's gotta be close," said Lorraine. "It's a street named after a tree, and all the streets in this neighborhood are named after trees."

"Locust is the name of a tree?" asked Janie. "I thought it was a bug."

Alex and Lorraine laughed. "It's also the name of a tree," they told Janie.

"The reason all the streets around here are named after trees is because this area is called Kingswood," explained Alex. "My dad says that he likes to think that we are living in the 'King's woods.' And since Jesus is the King of our lives, it means we're living in Jesus' woods!"

"That's pretty neat," Lorraine exclaimed. "I never would have thought of that!"

Just then, T-Bone, the family's black Labrador, came into the kitchen, trying to crowd up to the table with the girls.

"Oh, this dog!" Mother exclaimed. "He has been following me around all day. I think he's bored!"

"We'll entertain him, Mom," Alex volunteered. "Come on, T-Bone, we'll take you for a walk."

The big dog barked joyously and bounded to the front door. Alex ran to get his leash and snapped it onto his collar. T-Bone pulled Alex out of the door and led the girls down Juniper Street hill at a fast pace.

"Slow down, T-Bone!" Alex hollered. "You're gonna jerk my arm off!"

"Something tells me T-Bone is glad to get out of the house," laughed Janie.

"You can say that again!" Alex agreed. "Whoa, T-Bone!"

The walkers briskly moved on down the hill and around the curve to Maple Street. "There's creepy Julie's house," hissed Janie.

"I still can't believe she deserted us to be Melissa's friend," Lorraine said angrily.

Alex said nothing. She had been deeply hurt by Julie's actions. She did not want to talk about it.

They moved on up Maple Street, passing Walnut, Ash, and Elm Streets. They came to a busy intersection. On the

other side of the intersection was a park.

"Oh, let's take T-Bone to the park!" Janie cried.

"Okay," Alex agreed. "He would like that."

Alex pushed the button on the traffic light pole to stop the busy traffic. Automobiles screeched to a halt. The girls and T-Bone began to cross the street. All of a sudden T-Bone saw something that made him very excited.

On the other side of the street was a

female black Labrador. She looked straight at T-Bone and wagged her tail. Then she began to run across the street. As she streaked past T-Bone, she glanced over her shoulder and looked to see if T-Bone would follow her.

T-Bone did just that. Before Alex knew what was happening, the big dog jerked the leash from her hands and took off after the female dog.

"STOP!" Alex hollered. "T-BONE! COME BACK HERE!"

Just then, the traffic light changed to green. Cars began to move forward. Janie grabbed Alex and pulled her, along with Lorraine, to safety on the other side of the street. Alex gasped and watched in horror as T-Bone turned suddenly to come back across the street in front of the cars.

"T-BONE!" she screamed. "GO BACK! YOU'LL BE KILLED!"

CHAPTER 7

Dog in the Mall

Tires squealed and cars screeched to a stop, barely missing T-Bone and the female Labrador. The dogs, however, did not seem concerned. They scampered on across the street, past Alex, and into the park beyond.

"T-BONE!" Alex shouted, stamping her feet. "YOU COME HERE!" But the big dog continued to run with his new friend.

Alex, Janie, and Lorraine chased the dogs as fast as they could. The dogs led them out the other side of the park and into an unfamiliar neighborhood.

Alex felt her legs tire as she ran after T-Bone up one street and down another. Finally, the dogs halted in front of a small, white house. The female dog lay down on the front porch. T-Bone stood and gazed at her, as if he did not know what to do. Alex stumbled into the yard and grabbed T-Bone's leash.

"T-BONE, YOU BIG MUTT!" she gasped and sank down beside him for a rest. The big dog gave her face a lick.

"ACK!" Alex cried. "Keep your old slobbery kisses to yourself. I'm mad at you!" She stood up. "Come on, we'd better get out of this yard." Alex dragged T-Bone over to the sidewalk and down the street toward Janie and Lorraine, who had dropped far behind in the chase.

Janie had a few things to say to T-Bone. She was telling him how some people eat "dog stew" when she was suddenly interrupted.

"Hey, look!" Lorraine exclaimed, pointing to the street sign.

It took Alex and Janie awhile to figure out why Lorraine was so excited. The street sign said, "Locust Drive."

"Locust!" Alex cried. "That's Melissa's street."

Janie wasn't so sure. "The directory said 'Locust.' It didn't say 'Locust Drive,' " she pointed out.

"That's because there's not enough room in the directory to print the whole address," Alex told Janie.

"Well, then maybe 'Locust' means 'Locust Street' instead of 'Locust Drive,' " argued Janie.

"Let's look and see if Melissa's house is on this street," Alex suggested. "If it is, then we'll know she lives on Locust Drive."

"Okay," Janie agreed.

"Uh, does anybody remember the house number?" asked Lorraine.

"Oh, sure," Alex replied. "It was 6814 or 6815 or something like that."

"I think it was 6816," said Janie.

"Well, whatever." Alex led the way down Locust Drive. "Let's look for those numbers and then narrow it down."

"What do you mean 'narrow it down'?" Janie asked with a frown.

"We can look for a name on the mailbox or something," answered Alex.

The girls and T-Bone walked all the way to the end of the block. They stopped at a stoplight marking another busy intersection.

"Now what do we do?" Janie complained. "The street numbers on Locust Drive end with 6679. We didn't even come to the 6800s."

"I bet Locust continues on the other side of this intersection," Alex guessed, gazing across the busy street. She shaded her eyes with her hand. "Can anybody read the street sign over there?"

"I think it starts with an 'L,'" Lorraine answered.

"Maybe we shouldn't go any farther," Janie said. "We've walked a long ways. Does anybody have a watch? My mom wants me home by five."

Nobody had a watch.

"It can't be five yet," Alex insisted. "Let's cross the street and see if Locust Drive is on the other side. If it's not, we'll turn around and go back home."

"And what if it is?" Janie asked.

"If it is Locust Drive," Alex continued, "we'll find Melissa's house real fast and then turn around and go home."

When the traffic light turned green, the girls and T-Bone scampered across the busy street. On the other side, Alex was pleased to find that Locust Drive did indeed continue.

"See! What did I tell you?" Alex shouted joyfully. She began to skip down the street with T-Bone trotting beside her. Janie and Lorraine followed close behind.

Suddenly, Locust Drive bent sharply to the left. A street sign marked the bend, showing that the street was now called Sycamore Lane.

"Sycamore Lane!" Alex exclaimed. "What happened to Locust?"

"It disappeared!" Lorraine shouted.

"That's ridiculous." Janie stamped her foot.

"It's a short block," Alex observed. "I can see another street sign up the way. Let's go see if it turns back into Locust Drive."

The girls charged up the block. Sure enough, at the next bend in the road, the street sign again read, "Locust Drive."

"Come on!" Alex laughed. "Locust Drive goes up that hill. Last one up is a rotten egg!" She and T-Bone sprinted forward. Soon they were panting. The street was not very long, but it was very steep. Reaching the top of the hill, Alex came to an abrupt stop.

"Brussels sprouts!" she gasped. "Hey! Look at this!"she called.

"Guess I'm the rotten egg," Janie grumbled as she reached Alex a step or two behind Lorraine.

"WOW!" she cried, and so did Lorraine, when they saw what was on the other side of the hill.

Locust Drive plunged straight down and at its bottom sprawled the giant Kingswood Shopping Mall.

"Can you believe we just reached the mall?" Alex asked.

"We must be a long ways from home," Lorraine commented.

Janie and Alex stared at Lorraine.

"Uh, I think you're right, Lorraine," Alex slowly said. She turned around and looked behind her. "I'm not sure of the way back home."

"Neither am I," Janie said. "We've twisted and turned so much that I'm all mixed up on my directions."

"It's getting dark," Lorraine pointed out. "Look! The streetlights are turning on."

"It must be after five," Janie sighed. "I'm gonna be in big trouble."

"Sorry, Janie," Alex patted her best friend's shoulder.

"What do we do now?" Lorraine asked.

"Let me think." Alex held up her hand.

"I know!" she said after a moment's thought. "We'll go down to the mall, find a telephone, and call my mom. Then, she can pick us up."

"Great idea!" Janie and Lorraine agreed. The girls and T-Bone hurried down the hill. They ran through the parking lot to one of the mall entrances.

"See, there's the telephones," Alex announced as they stared through the glass double doors. "I'll just run inside and call my mom. You stay here with T-Bone." She gave Janie the dog's leash and hurried inside. A moment later, she returned with a sheepish look on her face.

"Uh, anybody got a quarter?" she asked.

"Oh, brother," Janie rolled her eyes skyward. She and Lorraine fished through their pockets. They both came up empty-handed.

"Now what do we do?" Janie wailed.

"Wait a minute, " Alex replied, trying to act calm. "Don't panic. We'll think of something."

The three girls sat down on the sidewalk outside the double doors to think. T-Bone patiently sat beside them.

"I've got it!" Lorraine suddenly cried.

Alex and Janie looked at her in surprise. Lorraine hardly ever came up with ideas.

"You know that little booth in the middle of the mall where a lady sits and helps you if you have any questions?"

"The Information Booth!" Alex and Janie cried together.

"Great idea, Lorraine!" Alex clapped her friend's back. "We can go there for help." She was so relieved that she swung Lorraine around in circles. This made T-Bone so excited that he barked and jumped until he became completely tangled in his leash.

"Who's going to stay outside with T-Bone?" Janie wondered.

Alex stared at Janie hopefully.

"Don't look at me. What if he decided to run away again? I couldn't catch him."

Alex turned to Lorraine.

"Oh, no," Lorraine cried. "I'm kind of scared of dogs."

"Okay," Alex sighed. "I'll stay outside with T-Bone. You two go to the Information Booth and call my mom."

"What? I can't call your mom and tell her to come and get us at the shopping mall," cried Janie. "She might yell at me."

"Then call your mom," said Alex.

"That's worse!" Janie retorted. "I *know* my mom would yell at me!"

"How about you, Lorraine? Would you call my mom?" Alex asked without much hope. Lorraine was much more timid than Janie.

Lorraine shook her head and looked down at the ground.

"Can't we all go in?" Janie pleaded. "Maybe no one would notice T-Bone."

Alex glanced at the giant black dog sitting beside her and laughed. "Are you kidding?" she asked Janie.

"It's too bad we don't have a stroller to

put T-Bone in," Lorraine giggled. "We could disguise him as a baby."

"Disguise him?" Alex repeated. A smile began to spread across her face. She took off her sweatshirt and slipped it over the dog's head. With quite a struggle, she managed to get his long legs through the armholes. She then tied the hood in place. T-Bone did not like the hood at all and shook his head from side to side.

"You might as well get used to the hood and stop shaking your head," Alex told the dog. She opened the doors to the mall. "Come on." She grinned as she led T-Bone inside.

Janie and Lorraine could not stop giggling. They followed Alex and T-Bone into the stream of people shopping in the mall.

"Hurry up," Alex called to them. "You need to walk on either side of T-Bone to help hide him."

"Oh, Alex!" Janie covered her face with her hands. "This is so embarrassing!"

Lorraine was embarrassed, too. She would not even look at the people who stopped and pointed at T-Bone.

Alex ignored the laughter and the stares of the people around them. She and the dog moved straight ahead as if it were the most natural thing in the world to bring a dog to a shopping mall.

"Uh oh, brussels sprouts!" Alex suddenly cried. "I see a policeman!"

"Where?" Janie and Lorraine asked together.

"Straight ahead," Alex replied, "and he's coming this way."

"What do we do?" her friends cried.

"Let's walk on the other side of this crowd of people," Alex directed. "Maybe the policeman won't see T-Bone."

The girls and the dog moved to the far side of a group of older women who were walking past a line of shops. Alex and T-Bone slowed their pace. So did Janie and Lorraine. T-Bone was well hidden behind large shopping bags and purses.

Everything might have gone well except that, at that moment, the group of shoppers was passing by a meat and cheese shop. The shop owner was just setting up a table full of sausage samples. The sausages had been freshly grilled and cut into bite-sized pieces for people to taste. There was one thing, however, that the owner of the shop had not taken into consideration. He had not counted on a dog passing by his display, and certainly not as big a dog as T-Bone.

T-Bone's nose was on the same level as the table of sausages. He could not help but smell the wonderful aroma of freshly cooked sausage. As soon as he reached the table, the dog could not resist snatching an entire plate of sausages. He wolfed it down before anyone could even think to try and stop him.

"HEY!" shouted the shop owner in surprise. "A DOG ATE MY SAUSAGES!"

For a quick moment, Alex stared into the angry eyes of the shop owner. She did not know what to say or do. But T-Bone, frightened by the shouts of the shop owner, did know what to do. Jerking his leash out of Alex's hands, the dog bounded away, a half-eaten sausage hanging from his mouth.

"SOMEBODY STOP THAT DOG!" the owner yelled.

In his haste, T-Bone bumped squarely into the group of older women. Purses and packages flew every which way.

"HELP! HELP!" the women cried.

"T-BONE!" Alex yelled. "COME BACK HERE!" Stumbling over purses and bags, Alex ran up the mall in pursuit of the big dog.

Suddenly the loud shriek of a police whistle sounded in Alex's ears.

"STOP!" hollered the policeman. "STOP AT ONCE!"

But Alex could not stop—at least not until she had caught T-Bone. She was afraid the dog might get hurt or someone might steal him or he might dash outside and be lost forever!

"STOP! STOP!" the policeman continued to shout. Alex cringed. She was in a lot of trouble now. Would she be arrested and put in jail?

CHAPTER 8

T-Bone's Disaster

Alex dodged shoppers, strollers, and small children as she sped down the center of the mall after T-Bone. Tripping over a shopping bag, Alex crashed into one woman, causing her to drop all of her packages..

"I'm sorry!" Alex called over her shoulder. She continued to chase after the dog.

T-Bone himself was causing quite an uproar. People quickly moved out of his way. Adults and children alike laughed and pointed at the big dog galloping through the shopping mall, dressed in Alex's sweatshirt.

"T-BONE! COME BACK!" Alex shouted again. She glanced back. The policeman was gaining on her.

Picking up speed, Alex nearly caught T-Bone who had slowed his pace to sniff the wonderful smells from a pizza stand.

"Now I've got you!" Alex gasped. She reached out to grab the dog's collar, but T-Bone did not want to be caught yet.

"COME BACK!" Alex wailed as the big dog bounded away. Suddenly, a giant hand gripped her shoulder. Looking up, Alex stared into the stern eyes of the policeman.

"Please, let me go," Alex squeaked. "I need to get my dog."

"We will get your dog in a minute," the policeman coolly replied. "First, I would like to know who you are."

"Uh, my name is Alex Brackenbury."

"Well, Alex Brackenbury," the policeman repeated, "don't you know that it's against the law to bring a dog into a shopping mall?"

Alex gulped, but before she could answer, a loud scream followed by a thunderous crash sounded from the pottery shop next door.

Alex and the policeman ran to see what was the matter. Looking in the door of the shop, Alex gasped in alarm. A giant display of dishes had somehow fallen, making a mountain of rubble.

Several customers stood pressed against the walls of the shop to avoid being hit by flying pieces of pottery. A salesclerk hid behind a counter.

Upon seeing Alex and the policeman, the clerk slowly stood up. The customers stepped away from the walls.

A sudden whimpering noise sounded in the rear of the store. A dining-room table stood at the back of the shop. The table was covered with a white lace tablecloth and was set with beautiful blue- and gold-tone pottery dishes. But the sight that made Alex's heart sink to the bottom of her toes was the dog's head peeking around the corner of the table.

"T-Bone," Alex sighed in frustration. "Come here!"

Immediately, Alex realized that it had been the wrong thing to say. Terribly frightened, T-Bone rushed to Alex's side. In doing so, his big, black tail caught on the lace tablecloth and pulled it along behind him. The tablecloth and dishes fell to the floor! CRASH! BAM!

Alex closed her eyes and held her hands over her ears. T-Bone whimpered at her side.

"GET THAT DOG OUT OF HERE!" the salesclerk screamed.

"You go sit over there on that bench," the policeman directed Alex, pointing to a bench not far from the pottery shop. "And take your dog with you!"

The policeman entered the shop to try and help the salesclerk. Alex and T-Bone shuffled to the bench and collapsed on it. T-Bone, knowing he had done something wrong, laid his head on Alex's lap.

"Alex!" someone whispered right behind her.

Alex turned her head. Janie and

Lorraine stood behind the bench.

"Did you see what T-Bone did?" Alex asked her friends.

"Yeah, we heard the crash," Janie replied, shaking her head.

"What's the policeman going to do?" asked Lorraine.

"I don't know, but I think we're in big trouble!" Alex stroked T-Bone's head. The dog looked mournfully up at her.

It wasn't long before custodians and security guards arrived at the pottery shop. The policeman approached the bench where Alex, T-Bone, Janie, and Lorraine sat.

"Are these your friends?" he asked Alex, pointing to Janie and Lorraine.

Alex nodded.

"Are any of your parents here in the mall?" he asked.

They shook their heads.

"Then all of you better come with me."

The girls and T-Bone followed the policeman into an office-lined hallway that ran off of the main section of the mall. The policeman led them into one of the offices.

Seating himself behind a desk, the policeman motioned the girls to sit on chairs. He leaned forward and stared at them.

"Did you girls know that it is against city law to bring an animal into a shopping mall?" the policeman asked.

No one answered right away. Alex looked at Janie and Lorraine. They had scrunched as far down in their chairs as possible and both stared at the floor. Alex knew it was up to her to answer the policeman's question.

"Uh, I knew we weren't *supposed* to bring a dog into the mall," Alex admitted to the policeman, "but I didn't know it was against the law."

"Why did you bring your dog into the mall?" the policeman asked.

"We were looking for the Information Booth," Alex answered. "We needed to call my mom but we didn't have a quarter for the pay phones." Alex went on to tell the policeman how they had been lost and had decided to call Alex's mom from the shopping mall.

"I'm awfully sorry," Alex ended. "I didn't mean for T-Bone to eat all those sausages or break all those dishes."

Turning to her dog, Alex scolded, "T-Bone! If you'd keep your nose out of things, you wouldn't get into so much trouble!"

A chuckle escaped the lips of the policeman. Becoming serious again, he said, "Even though you did not mean for it to happen, your dog has done considerable damage to someone else's property. You also have broken a city ordinance by letting the dog into the mall. I'm afraid I will have to call all of your parents."

Janie and Lorraine gasped in alarm. Alex was not surprised. She had already figured that her parents would be called because of the damage T-Bone had done.

The girls gave the policeman their telephone numbers and waited nervously while he called their parents. Within minutes, the three sets of parents arrived at the mall.

"Oh, Alex, we were so worried about you!" cried Mother as soon as she saw Alex. "Why didn't you call home?"

"That's why we came into the mall in the first place," Alex tried to explain. "We were going to call you. . . ."

"Because we got lost and couldn't find

our way back home," Janie interrupted.

"Because T-Bone started chasing another dog and led us far away from our neighborhood," Lorraine added.

"And because *someone* just had to follow Locust Drive to find Melissa's house," said Janie, giving Alex an exasperated look.

"You wanted to find her house, too!" Alex snapped at Janie.

"GIRLS! GIRLS!" the policeman held up his hands. "Let's tell the story one at a time. Alex, you go first."

A few chuckles came from the grown-ups when they heard how T-Bone had snatched the sausages. But when Lorraine finished the story by telling how T-Bone had smashed the dishes in the pottery shop, no one laughed. The only noise was a loud groan from Alex's father. "I guess we had better go look at the damage," he said.

The grown-ups walked down the mall to the pottery shop. Alex and T-Bone stayed behind with Janie and Lorraine. Alex had no desire to see the salesclerk again—ever!

When her parents returned, all that Alex's father said was, "Most of it should be covered by insurance."

After promising the policeman that they would never again bring a dog into the shopping mall, the girls left with their parents. Alex waved good-bye to Janie and Lorraine as she climbed into the back-seat of her family's car.

Alex's father did not start the car right away. Instead, he turned around and looked at Alex as she sat in the backseat of the family station wagon.

"You know, Firecracker," said Father, "bringing T-Bone into the mall was the wrong thing to do."

"Boy, do I!" Alex muttered. She put an arm around T- Bone, who sat next to her. "I promise that I will never take you into a shopping mall again," she whispered. T-Bone gave her face a grateful lick.

"What you may not know," Father continued speaking to Alex, "is that, legally, your mother and I are not responsible for any of the damage that T-Bone did to the pottery shop."

"You aren't?" Alex was surprised.

"No," Father replied. "It was your fault that the dog broke the pottery because it was you who let him into the mall. But you do not have to pay for the damage because children cannot be sued in court. The law also says that parents cannot be sued for the damage caused by their children. So, according to the law, we don't have to pay for it either."

"You don't?" Alex's face brightened. Maybe her parents would not be so upset with her if they didn't have to pay for the broken dishes.

"However," Father continued, "I do not choose to live according to the world's law. I choose, instead, to live under God's law."

Alex held her breath and stared at her father. She wondered if God had some special law for children and dogs who broke pottery.

"Jesus gave us two laws to live by," Father told Alex. "One law is to love God with all of your heart and the other is to love your neighbor as yourself."

Alex nodded her head. She remembered hearing that verse before.

Father leaned across the front seat of the car and stared into Alex's eyes. "Do you think that we would be loving our neighbor if we did not pay for the dishes that our dog broke?"

"No, I guess not," answered Alex. "But you said the insurance would pay for it."

"I think insurance will pay for most of it, but not all of it."

"How much do you think it will pay for?" asked Alex.

"Well," Father rubbed his chin, "I would estimate that T-Bone did at least one thousand dollars worth of damage in that store."

"A thousand dollars!" Alex exclaimed.

"The plates that he pulled off of the table cost fifty dollars a piece."

"Brussels sprouts!" Alex cried. "Who would buy fifty-dollar plates?"

"No one with a dog like T-Bone," said Mother, joining in the conversation.

"I don't know how much the insurance will pay," Father went on, "but I think we should pay for whatever amount it does not cover. I guess that it could be several hundred dollars."

Alex bit her lip. "I guess I should help pay for it since it was my fault," she volunteered.

"Yes, I think you should," Father said.

"I have sixty dollars at home that I was saving up for a new ten-speed bicycle," Alex told her father. "You can have that."

"All right," said Father, "and I will withhold your allowance for a while."

"Okay," Alex sighed and flopped back against the seat. She would never NEVER take a dog into the mall again.

CHAPTER 9

Forgive Julie?

Alex had quite a surprise waiting for her when she arrived at school the next morning. A group of girls waited for her in front of the classroom door. It was the same group that had not spoken to her for the past several days. But today they wore friendly smiles.

"Hi, Alex." One of the girls stepped forward. "We're sorry that we were so mean to you."

"Yes, and we hope you will forgive us," said another.

"We made this card for you," still another girl said and handed Alex a brightly decorated, homemade card. On the inside it said, "Let's be friends again."

All of the girls had signed it.

Alex was so shocked that the only thing she could say was, "Brussels sprouts!"

The girls laughed. They turned to go into the classroom.

Alex started to follow when she heard, as if coming out of nowhere, someone whisper, "Alex! Psssst, Alex!"

Alex glanced up and down the hallway. No one was in sight.

"Alex! Over here!" hissed the voice.

Alex looked quickly to her left. The voice was coming from a side entryway. Cautiously, Alex tiptoed to the entryway and peeked around its corner.

Her eyes met the eyes of the one person she did not want to see—Julie! Alex quickly turned around and hurried back toward her classroom.

"Alex, wait! Please come back!" called Julie.

Alex stopped and stood still in the middle of the hall.

"Please, Alex, will you forgive me?" Julie pleaded.

Alex did not answer. She knew she should forgive Julie, but she was still very mad at her for becoming one of Melissa's followers. Traitor! Julie was a traitor!

Alex might have stood in the hall all morning not knowing what to do, but suddenly the late bell rang, reminding both girls that they were supposed to be in their classrooms. Alex hurried to her room. So did Julie.

"Alex, you are late!" Mrs. Hibbits told her as soon as she entered the room.

"I'm sorry," Alex apologized. She rushed to her desk.

"You know the rule, Alex," said Mrs. Hibbits, tapping her foot. "You will have to get a tardy slip from the office."

Alex stomped out of the room and down the hallway to the school office. She was doubly angry at Julie now. She had caused Alex to get her first tardy slip of the year. Julie would be lucky if Alex spoke to her again—EVER!

When Alex stepped into the office, an all-too-familiar voice said, "Hi, Alex." It was Julie! She had to get a tardy slip, too.

Alex sat down as far away from Julie as she could get to wait for her late pass. She folded her arms across her chest and refused to look in Julie's direction.

"Alex, please talk to me," Julie begged. But Alex did not. She continued to stare straight ahead. She wished the secretary would hurry up. She wanted to get away from Julie and back to class.

"What are you girls doing here?" a loud voice suddenly asked.

Alex sighed heavily. It was Mrs. Larson. Alex had hoped that the principal would not see her.

"I was late to class," Alex explained.

"So was I," said Julie.

"You girls must have been late together," Mrs. Larson guessed. "Am I right?"

Alex shrugged her shoulders. She did not know how to tell Mrs. Larson that she was not speaking to Julie.

"I guess we were sort of together," Julie volunteered in a small voice. "It was my fault that we were late."

Mrs. Larson looked at Julie and at Alex for what seemed a long time. Then, without saying a word, she pulled out a notepad and began to write.

"Julie, here is your tardy slip," Mrs. Larson said. "You may go back to class."

Mrs. Larson looked at Alex as soon as Julie had left the room. "I thought you and Julie were good friends," she said.

"Not anymore," Alex replied gruffly. "She decided to be Melissa's friend. I am not speaking to her!"

"Isn't that what the other girls did to you?" asked Mrs. Larson. "Are you going to treat Julie in the same way that they treated you?"

"That's different!" Alex replied. She took her tardy slip and left the office. She felt the principal's eyes on her back as she walked down the hall.

"Mrs. Larson can say what she wants," Alex told herself. "But I don't have to be friends with Julie if I don't want to. If she wanted to be my friend, she shouldn't have left me to be Melissa's friend."

Alex tried to forget about Julie, but all day, she was bothered by thoughts of her. Later at home, Alex tried to clear her mind of thoughts of Julie. She was in her room, finishing up her math homework when someone knocked on her door.

"Come in," Alex responded.

The door opened. Father entered the room and sat down on the bed.

Alex held her breath. Father had not yet told Alex what her punishment would be for taking T-Bone into the shopping mall.

"As you know, Firecracker," began Father, "bringing a dog into the mall is a serious offense."

Alex felt her heart sink to her toes. She would probably be grounded for a year.

"If the same situation were to happen

again, would you handle it any differently?" Father asked.

"Oh, yes," Alex answered immediately. "If I could do it all over again, I would either talk Janie or Lorraine into staying outside with T-Bone, or else have one of them call their own mother."

"Well, I'm glad to see that you learned something from it all," said Father, looking pleased.

"Oh, yeah," Alex replied. "I wish I'd never taken T-Bone into the shopping mall. I didn't mean for him to break all those dishes."

"I know you didn't intend for it to happen, Firecracker," said Father, "and intent is very important. It says in the Bible that God looks at the intentions of our hearts. That means He is as concerned with what we mean to do as with what we do."

Father smiled at Alex and continued, "So, if my heavenly Father considers the intentions of His children, then I, as a

Christian father, need to consider the intentions of my children, don't I?"

Alex nodded hopefully. Maybe she wouldn't be grounded for a year.

"Because I know your intentions were good," he said, "I'm only going to ground you for one week."

"Whew!" Alex breathed a sigh of relief. She hugged her father. "I'm glad you are a Christian father," she told him.

Father laughed and hugged her back.

After Father left the room, Alex lay on

her bed and stared at the ceiling. Her father always seemed to do the right thing. That was probably because he tried to live the way the Bible said to live. And that's what she would do, too.

Alex started to jump off the bed. But a disturbing thought made her stop. What about forgiveness? God said you needed to forgive the people who hurt you. What about Julie? If she was going to live by the Bible, shouldn't she forgive Julie?

"Brussels sprouts!" Alex muttered. She would take her bath now and think about forgiving Julie later.

Gathering her pajamas and robe together, Alex headed for the bathroom. But when she got there, she found she could not take a bath at all. Neither could anyone else. The floor of the tub was littered with a jumble of plumbing parts and tools.

"Sorry, Firecracker," Father mumbled around a screw that he held between his teeth. "You will have to use the other bathroom. I have to fix this faucet before your mother does something drastic like call a plumber."

Alex sighed and shook her head. The last time Father had "fixed" the faucet, the "hot" water had run cold and the "cold" water had run hot. She wondered what else could go wrong.

After her bath, Alex curled up in bed. She was getting ready to read a chapter in her Bible when a sudden uproar sounded outside her bedroom door.

Leaping out of bed, Alex ran to see what was happening. She met Barbara and Rudy in the hallway. They, too, had heard the noise. It was coming from the bathroom. The three children hurried to peek in the doorway.

Father stood in the tub surrounded by plumbing tools and parts. He stared up into the shower head. An exasperated look covered his face.

Mother stood beside the tub. Her hands were on her hips. She did not look very happy. "What do you mean the shower won't work?" she demanded.

"It just won't work!" Father exclaimed. "Look! Look at the faucet! It's turned on but no water is flowing out of the shower."

Barbara, Alex, and Rudy exchanged sighs. "Hey, Dad," Rudy said, "maybe if you turn the faucet off, the shower will work!"

"Very funny," Father mumbled. He fiddled a little longer with the shower head, first turning one screw and then another. Still, nothing happened.

"Well, I might as well quit for the night." Father reached for the faucet and turned the water off.

"AHHHHHH!" He screamed in surprise. Water shot out of the shower head, drenching him completely. Quickly, Father turned the faucet to what used to be the "on" position. The water stopped.

Barbara, Alex, and Rudy burst into loud laughter. But no one laughed louder than Mother.

When Alex returned to her bedroom, she heard Father say to Mother, "Okay, okay, you can call a plumber."

Good! Alex grinned to herself. It would be nice to have a proper shower. Then she would not have to rescue Rudy from water that was too hot.

Snuggling under the covers, Alex reached for her Bible. She opened it to the Book of Matthew and began reading where she had left off the night before: "Your heavenly Father will forgive you if you forgive those who sin against you; but if you refuse to forgive them, he will not forgive you."

"Uh oh!" Alex immediately thought of Julie. Was the Lord telling her that He wanted her to forgive Julie?

"If You want me to forgive her, Lord, I'll try," Alex prayed out loud. "But I'm still awfully mad at her. Please help me. Amen."

CHAPTER 10

Friends Again

A loud clinking noise woke Alex the next morning. It sounded as if someone outside her bedroom door was beating on a metal pipe with a hammer. "CLINK! CLINK! CLUNK!" went the awful noise.

Alex rolled out of bed and stumbled to the bathroom.

"Well, hello, young lady," said a strange man in answer to Alex's surprised look. The man was standing in the bathtub and knocking on the faucet with a screwdriver.

"Can't seem to get this thing loose," he mumbled. "Somebody jammed it on real tight."

Taking two steps at a time, Alex hurried down the stairs to the kitchen.

"Who's the stranger in the bathroom?" Alex asked her mother.

Father sat at the kitchen table, sipping his coffee. He groaned at Alex's question. "That is the plumber," he told her. "Your mother does not waste time."

Mother winked at Alex. "I had to get a plumber in here quickly before your father tried to fix the shower again."

Alex giggled at the look that crossed her father's face. He pretended to be very hurt by Mother's remark.

Alex was in a merry mood when she walked to school with Janie that morning. This was sure to be a good day. The shower would be fixed, she was only grounded for a week, and the girls at school were her friends again. Things were definitely looking up.

However, when Alex got to school, she found that everything was not quite as she had expected. The usual groups of girls lined the fifth- and sixth-grade hallway. But today, no one smiled at Alex or waved to her as they had yesterday. In fact, the girls in her class became very quiet when Alex passed them. Alex noticed that Melissa was back and was the center of attention.

"Oh, no," Alex whispered to Janie. "Do you think the girls are going to be mean to me again now that Melissa is back?"

At morning recess, Alex, Janie, and Lorraine suddenly found themselves surrounded by fifth-grade girls. Neither Melissa nor Crystal were among them. Julie was there but hung back from the main crowd.

"Melissa and Crystal said that you were the one that messed up the girls' bathroom," one girl accused Alex.

"What?" Alex was stunned. Surely, she hadn't heard that right.

"That's ridiculous!" Janie hollered. "Alex did not do it."

"Were you there?" a girl asked Janie.

"No, but . . . " Janie began.

"Then be quiet!"

"Melissa said that you told Mrs. Larson that she and Crystal damaged the bathroom so that they would get in trouble," the first girl said to Alex.

"Yeah, so everyone would think that Melissa and Crystal were the bad ones," added another girl.

"And so that we would all become your friends again," said a third.

Alex stared at the girls with her mouth wide open. She could hardly believe her ears. Feeling her face turn several different colors of red, Alex was just about to tell the girls that she did not care to be friends with people who believed that she damaged property and then told lies about it, when Julie suddenly pushed her way to the center of the group.

"That is the dumbest thing I ever heard!" Julie hollered. "We all know Alex. We know that she wouldn't stop up the sinks in the girls' bathroom. And we know that she doesn't tell lies either. Melissa's the one that's telling the lies. She's been lying to you all along. And you're stupid if you still listen to her!"

Julie glanced quickly at Alex. "I don't blame Alex if she never forgives any of us!" she added. And with that, Julie ran off, hurriedly brushing tears from her eyes.

A heavy silence fell upon the girls. Julie had said it all.

Alex left the group and followed Julie. She caught up with her near the softball diamond.

"Thanks for sticking up for me back there," Alex said to Julie.

"Oh, sure," Julie wiped her eyes. "I'm really sorry about everything."

"That's okay," Alex shrugged. She stuck out her hand. "Friends?" she asked.

Julie grabbed her hand and shook it. "Friends!" she agreed with a grateful smile.

At lunchtime, Alex invited Julie to join her and Janie and Lorraine at their table

at the back of the cafeteria. They were all
very surprised when the other fifth- grade
girls began to fill up the empty spaces
around the table.

"We decided that Julie was right," one
girl explained to Alex.

"Yeah, we don't know why we ever
listened to Melissa," said another.

"We're not going to listen to her again!"
declared a third.

"We're really sorry, Alex. We hope we
can all be friends again," a fourth girl said.

"Sure we can," Alex generously replied. She smiled at everybody.

"I feel a lot better now that everything's right again," one of the girls commented.

"You mean now that we're not listening to Melissa's gossip," another one pointed out.

"My mom said that gossip is like poison and whenever you listen to it, the poison spreads to you," Alex told them.

"I think she's right!" someone exclaimed. "At first it was kind of fun to listen to the gossip, but then later on, I started feeling really bad."

"Why did you stop speaking to me in the first place?" Alex asked them.

"It's really stupid," one of the girls warned.

"Tell me anyway," pleaded Alex.

"Melissa said that you take showers with your brother!" someone answered.

"What?" Alex cried.

"With Rudy?" Janie asked. She and Lorraine began to giggle.

"Why would Melissa say something like that?" Alex wondered.

"She said that when she spent the night at your house, you went into the bathroom when your brother was taking a shower. You stayed in there for a while and when you came back out, your hair was wet," the girls told Alex.

Alex frowned and tried to remember. All of a sudden, a light dawned in her eyes.

"Of course!" Alex cried. She began to giggle and giggle. Soon, she had everyone else at the table giggling.

"What's so funny?" they all finally gasped.

"It's all my dad's fault!" Alex began to explain. "See, we had this leaky shower faucet . . . "

Alex went on to tell the girls how the "hot" water ran cold and the "cold" water ran hot. She then told them how Rudy could not remember which way to turn the faucet and how he had to be "rescued" whenever he got the water too hot.

"I remember now that I had to help Rudy with the water when Melissa was at my house," Alex said.

"You mean that's what caused all this trouble?" Janie exclaimed. "How ridiculous!"

"You're right," the girls admitted.

"How about a peace offering?" someone suggested. A small package was thrown at Alex from a lunch sack.

"Sunflower seeds!" Alex chuckled.

Lorraine laughed and held out her hand. So did all the other girls. Alex shook a few seeds into the open hands. That left only a few for her but she didn't mind. She had her friends back again and the gossip was over.

Amen.

FRENCH FRY FORGIVENESS

Two Alexandrias!

Alex (short for Alexandria) expects to make new friends when she joins the swim team—but she doesn't count on meeting *another* Alexandria! How can she make friends with Alexandria, who pushes her into the pool for no reason?

Alex knows she should forgive Alexandria, but that seems impossible! Is there *anything* Alex can do to win Alexandria's friendship?

Every kid gets into the predicaments that Alex does—ones that start out small and mushroom. Readers will learn from Alex's mistakes and understand that they have the same sources of help that she turns to: A God who loves them and wants to help them, and parents who understand.

Other books in the Alex Series . . .

1 *Shoelaces and Brussels Sprouts*—It's always better to tell the truth, as Alex learns the hard way.

3 *Hot Chocolate Friendship*—Is winning first place as important to Alex as being a friend?

4 *Peanut Butter and Jelly Secrets*—Obeying her parents (even in little things) beats the awful results of disobeying.

NANCY LEVENE, who shares Alex's love of softball, lives with her husband and daughter in Kansas.

HOT CHOCOLATE FRIENDSHIP

The worst possible partner!

That's who Alex gets for the biggest project of the school year. She won't have a chance at first place if she has to work with Eric Linden. He's the slowest kid in third grade.

Alex can't understand why he has to be her partner. Is she supposed to share God's love with Eric? Could that be more important than winning first place?

Every kid gets into the predicaments that Alex does—ones that start out small and mushroom. Readers will learn from Alex's mistakes and understand that they have the same sources of help that she turns to: A God who loves them and wants to help them, and parents who understand.

Other books in the Alex Series . . .

1 *Shoelaces and Brussels Sprouts*—It's always better to tell the truth, as Alex learns the hard way.

2 *French Fry Forgiveness*—Sometimes making friends is harder than making enemies.

4 *Peanut Butter and Jelly Secrets*—Obeying her parents (even in little things) beats the awful results of disobeying.

NANCY LEVENE, who shares Alex's love of softball, lives with her husband and daughter in Kansas.